KU-178-806

The Dame

Grofield novels
by Donald E. Westlake,
writing as Richard Stark

The Damsel

The Dame

The Blackbird

Lemons Never Lie

The Dame

A Grofield Novel

Donald E. Westlake

writing as Richard Stark

A Foul Play Press Book

The Countryman Press, Inc.
Woodstock, Vermont

Copyright © 1969 by Richard Stark

This edition first published in 1990 by Foul Play Press, an imprint of
The Countryman Press, Inc., Woodstock, Vermont 05091.

ISBN 0-88150-182-4

All rights reserved

Printed in the United States of America

10 9 8 7 6 5 4 3 2

to Parker

THE DAME

1

GROFIELD, not knowing what it was all about, got off the plane and walked through the sun into the main terminal building. He was at Isla Verde International Airport in San Juan, Puerto Rico, with sunshine and sea breezes sweeping through the open walls.

He got his suitcase and went down a flight of steps to the circular counter of the car-rental agency. "I'm supposed to pick up a car here," he told a clerk with a ferocious mustache. "The name's Wilcox." That was the name the letter had told him to use.

The clerk pointed a triumphant finger at Grofield's forehead. "Yes, *sir!* You been expected." He was beside himself with joy. He bustled away, bustled back again, and plunked a set of keys on the counter. "Everything's taken care of, sir. You'll find all the paperwork in the glove compartment."

"Thank you."

"And I'm supposed to give you this."

Another envelope. Grofield took it, thanked him again, and

went out to the parking lot to look for the car with the same license number as this set of keys.

It turned out to be a pale-blue Ford, two-door. The odometer registered a little over thirty-two hundred miles, and there was rust already on the bumpers. That would be the sea air at work.

Grofield dropped the new envelope on the seat beside him and checked out the glove compartment first, but the only things in there were a Texaco map of the island and the form he should show if required to demonstrate he had this car legally.

The envelope, when he opened it, contained nothing but a sheet of white paper folded once. Inside were typewritten instructions:

> 26 and 3 to Loiza
> 185 past Toma de Agua
> first left after 954
> .4 mile, turn right

Well, that was terse enough. Grofield opened the map, saw that Loiza was eighteen kilometers west of where he was now, and did some figuring in his head to turn eighteen kilometers into just over eleven miles. Toma de Agua was three kilometers south of Loiza, which was just under two miles, but how far was "past"? And how far to that first left after 954, which itself was past Toma de Agua?

Maybe another mile at the most. Figure a top of fourteen miles. To what? Home base, or just another letter?

There was only one way to find out. Grofield started the car, backed it out of the slot, and headed it up-ramp.

The airport roads were neat and broad, surrounded by green lawn. There was a lot of traffic, most of it ramshackle cars with here and there a ramshackle truck. Grofield had supposed he'd lose them all once he turned left away from the main San Juan highway, but a lot of them took the turn-off with him, and when the road narrowed from four lanes to two he found himself in the middle of an apparently endless line of slow-moving traffic. The road made sweeping curves back and forth, as though it had been designed by a water skier, and while at times it was straight enough to give the occasional Mercedes a shot at moving forward one place in line, Grofield and his Ford had no choice but to suffer in silence.

After a mile or two the exotic jungle greenery flanking the road became repetitious and dull, and the occasional poverty-row hut he passed looked the same as marginal living anywhere else in the tropics. There was no radio in the Ford, so Grofield had nothing to do but keep telling himself all this couldn't possibly be a practical joke. Nobody pays your air fare from Brownsville, Texas, to Houston, Texas, to San Juan, Puerto Rico, as part of a practical joke. Somewhere, somehow, behind it all somebody had to be wanting something, and they damn well had to be serious about it.

Two days ago Grofield had been in Matamoros, Mexico, across the Rio Grande from Brownsville. He had been in a green and shady hotel room, saying protracted farewells to a lovely young damsel named Elly, when a knock at the door had introduced a chinless, nervous, brown-skinned little man with an envelope containing a message from General Pozos. General Pozos was a banana-republic dictator whose life Grofield had inadvertently saved not long before, and now the General wanted a favor. The note had been ink-smeared and terse:

"You can perhaps help an acquaintance of mine. There will be profit in it."

With the note had come the airline tickets and instructions to present himself as Wilcox to the car-rental desk in San Juan.

He had not taken to the proposal at once. In the first place he was on his way home to see his wife, a patient girl from whom he had been separated too long. In the second place he had a suitcase full of money to transport, the result of a previous profitable expedition. In the third place he already had two occupations, actor and thief, neither of which seemed to be called for in this note, and he was not anxious to moonlight.

But what did they want? Who was the "acquaintance" of General Pozos? Where was the profit to come from? What was to be expected from him? The chinless messenger knew nothing, and said so.

"If it's the money that's bothering you," Elly had finally said while he paced the floor torn between inertia and curiosity, "I'll bring it to your wife myself."

"Ho ho," Grofield had said. "I'm afraid my wife wouldn't understand."

"You mean you're afraid she would."

"Whatever you like."

"I'll wear support stockings," Elly had volunteered.

Grofield had stopped his pacing to look at her. "You'll do what? Why?"

"Then she'll feel sorry for me."

You couldn't argue with logic like that. So Grofield's money was on its way to Grofield's wife in Pennsylvania via Elly, and Grofield himself was on his way to someplace "past" Toma de Agua via Ford.

Route 185 was unmarked. When he saw the road leading off to the left for San Isidro, Grofield understood he'd overshot. Cursing in English, he made a U turn that caused brakes to squeal in both directions, drove back to the road he wanted, made a left through the endless belt of eastbound traffic, and found himself on a narrow, deserted road flanked by grimy small shacks, many with crumbled automobiles decaying in their front yards.

Toma de Agua was merely a place where you could buy beer. Grofield curved around a drunk or two, drove on out of town, found his left and entered a road that almost immediately gave up its gritty blacktop in favor of dirt, reduced itself from two lanes to one, and began to climb. The foliage was more and more junglelike, dense, damp, dark green.

There were no more shacks after the blacktop gave out, no more signs of man at all, with the single exception of the road, which twisted and curved like a snake and kept pushing at violent angles uphill.

Four-tenths of a mile, the instructions had read. As a part of the ambivalence native to Puerto Rico the roads were marked in kilometers but the automobile odometers registered in miles.

Grofield kept an eye on the odometer in the Ford, and after the fourth tenth had clicked over he started looking for somewhere to turn right.

He almost missed it. Broad-leafed tree branches hung down on both sides, shadow from the overhanging foliage filled the empty spaces, and instead of a fully cleared dirt road there were only two dirt lines leading in. He hit the brakes, looked at it, decided there was nothing else that could be his right turn, and backed up slightly to get a better approach.

There was no sun in here; the snarled tree branches were too thick above to let in anything but a vague gray-green light. It was cool, with a dampness like fresh-turned earth. Flat thick leaves flapped at the Ford's windshield as Grofield followed the faint indications of a passage through the jungle.

At first this path—it couldn't really be counted a road—dipped downhill, but then it curved to the left and began to climb, even more steeply than the other road. Grofield drove in low gear, his left foot constantly twitching over the brake pedal.

He caught glimpses of white, then nothing, then more glimpses of white, then abruptly the house.

It was such a surprise that he took his foot off the gas and began at once to roll backward. He accelerated again, back into the clearing, and came to a stop in front of the house.

Villa. Not house—villa. Two stories high, broad across the front, with railed terraces fronting the set-back second floor. The whole thing was stucco, painted a blinding white in the sun.

And there was sun here, pouring down out of a royal-blue sky. The house had been built on cleared land on a knob of hill. Jungle was a restless green mass all around, but the house itself was graced by neat tropical gardens and a drive-way of raked stones. There was a complex high stone fountain in the center of the gardens in front of the house, a confusing array of fishes and cherubim, but the water was off now, leaving them all in postures that had no reason, and the chubby naked bodies in black stone looked like a bad joke in the middle of this riot of jungle growth, the gardens ablaze with flowers of red and orange, purple and yellow and white.

Grofield started across the driveway of stones toward the main entrance, but when the door opened down there he stopped. Two men came out and headed in his direction, both natives, both dressed in dirty white, both wearing straw hats. One carried a shotgun at port arms. The other was barely controlling a huge German shepherd on a taut leash.

Grofield kicked the gear lever into reverse, but there was no point in it. There was no room to turn the car around, and it would be impossible to back it all the way down that trail. The only way out was straight ahead, around the curve past the house and back to the trail from the other side, and that would mean driving through the welcoming committee with its shotgun and dog. If he was sure it was trouble, that's what he'd do, but right now he wasn't sure of anything.

Feeling strongly the absence of a gun of his own, Grofield put the Ford in neutral, left the motor running, and got out of the car to see what would happen next.

2

"Hello, Fido," Grofield said.

The dog looked at his throat.

The man with the shotgun said, "What you want here?"

"I was sent for."

"What your name?"

"Depends. Sometimes it's Wilcox. Does that ring a bell?"

It didn't. They looked blankly at one another. The dog kept looking at Grofield's throat.

Grofield said, "On the other hand, sometimes my name is Grofield. That any better?"

It was. The shotgun man nodded. "Hands on car," he said.

"What say?"

"Hands on car!" He seemed excitable.

"Oh," Grofield said. "Hands on car." He turned and faced the car, put his palms on its hot blue top. "Like so?"

The shotgun man came around behind him and frisked him, thoroughly and at length, until Grofield finally asked him, "What are you looking for—fleas?"

The shotgun man grunted, stopped patting Grofield's body, and said something in Spanish to the dog man. Puerto Rican Spanish was different from Mex, faster and harsher, with more of a rattle in it. Not that it made any difference to Grofield; there wasn't any breed of Spanish he understood.

The dog man rattled something back at the shotgun man. They both seemed irritated, and the irritation came through just as well in English when the shotgun man poked Grofield in the back with his shotgun and said, "Turn around, you."

Grofield turned around, putting his hands at his sides. The Ford engine was still purring away to itself, and the driver's door was still open, a quick step to Grofield's right.

The shotgun man said, "Why you no got a gun?"

It was an amazing question. Grofield said, "I didn't know I was supposed to have one."

The dog man rattled off another comment. The shotgun man shrugged, studied Grofield doubtfully, shrugged again, said something irritable out of the side of his mouth in Spanish, and then told Grofield, "You wait here."

"Whatever you say."

"You damn right."

The shotgun man went away, not quite moving at a swagger. The dog man stayed where he was, watching Grofield with flat mistrust. The German shepherd continued to study Grofield's throat.

Grofield's cigarettes were in his shirt pocket. He took them out now, aware of how much the movement made the dog man tense up, was elaborately casual about lighting one for himself, then extended the pack toward the dog man. The dog man shook his head, fast and brief. He was really very nervous, and Grofield hoped he wasn't nervous enough to drop the leash by mistake.

"Hi!"

It was a woman's voice, somewhat brassy, shouting from the direction of the house. Grofield and the dog man both looked in that direction, but Grofield couldn't see anyone there. The house was white and wide and sunlit, with no one visible.

The woman's voice called, "Come on up!" Then something in Spanish, then "It's okay. The dog won't do anything."

Grofield wasn't so sure. But the sentence in Spanish had apparently told the dog man to lay off. Without another look at Grofield he now trudged away, pulling the dog along with him. The dog didn't want to go at first, didn't want to stop his dispassionate consideration of Grofield's throat, but after he'd been tugged a few steps he turned obediently and went padding away at the side of his master.

Grofield reached into the Ford and cut the ignition, then pocketed the keys, shut the door, and walked on up to the house, the stones crunching beneath his feet. Now that he had leisure to notice the weather he became aware that it was hot out here under the sun, a good twenty degrees or more hotter than it had been in the leafy shade of the jungle.

"Hi!" called the woman's voice again. "Up here!"

Grofield looked up, and this time he saw her, indistinct in one of the second-story windows. He could tell nothing about her except that her arm was tanned and slender as she waved at him. He waved back and said, "How are things up there?"

"I'll meet you downstairs," she said, which wasn't an answer. "Lovely."

There was a slate-floored verandah across the front of the house, bare of furniture. Grofield crossed this, opened a screen door, and entered a cool dim world with thick white walls. Green and leafy plants grew all around, in pots on shelves, in planters on the floor. It was almost like being back in the jungle again, combined with an atmosphere reminiscent of a mission in southern California.

Arched doorways led away in three directions, into rooms equally cool and white-walled and dim. Grofield glanced through the doorways but stayed where he was, standing in the square anteroom on a dark Persian rug, admiring the heavy black iron ceiling fixture.

The woman came in from the doorway on the right. "Mr. Grofield," she said. "Thank you for coming."

She was deceptive, particularly here with the light slightly dim. She had a twenty-five-year-old body, appropriately dressed in white canvas slacks and bright-striped cotton top, with white sandals on bare feet. But the voice was somewhat older than that, a little rough, a little too used to late hours and neat whiskey and chain smoking. The hair was blond, but not too blond, cut medium short and done in the kind of casual way that takes a lot of time and attention.

The hair was a match for the body, but the face matched the voice. Over a conventionally pretty oval face time had etched lines and individuality and character. The face said "I am independent but not tough, aware but not cynical, strong but not belligerent, cautious but not frightened."

Grofield, in the first quick seconds of seeing her coming through the arched doorway, estimated her to be a rich forty. You couldn't be forty that well without spending a lot of money on the project, but you couldn't have that face and voice without being forty.

Answering her greeting, he said, "It's curiosity that brought me this far. No promises yet about anything else."

"Of course. My name is Belle Danamato. And you're Alan Grofield."

She had extended a hand, and when Grofield took it he found it firm and slender, the fingers soft. Someone else washed Belle Danamato's dishes. He said, "My pleasure, Miss Danamato."

"Mrs.," she said, and her mouth twisted as she added, "Not that that means anything."

"Domestic trouble?" Grofield asked. "Because if it is—"

The twisted mouth converted to a twisted smile and she shook her head, saying, "Not domestic trouble, Mr. Grofield. Not the way you mean. I wouldn't be coming to a man like you if that's all it was."

"A man like me," Grofield echoed. "I'm wondering what that's supposed to be."

"A man who comes here," she said, "without knowing why he's been summoned. Shall we sit indoors or out?"

"Your pleasure," Grofield said.

"The court is always nice in the afternoon."

She gestured toward the middle archway, and Grofield gestured back for her to lead the way. There was something slightly flirtatious about the way she smiled and nodded her head and stepped past him, but whether it was intentional or merely habit Grofield couldn't tell.

The archway led them into a broad underfurnished room with a gleaming floor of broad polished planks. A representational tapestry—man on burro—hung on the wall to the left. Heavy wooden chests and tables bore iron candelabra, stone figurines, more plants. Opposite, a row of curtained French doors was dappled with sunlight.

Belle Danamato walked across to the nearest French doors, her sandals slapping against the floor. When she opened the door, Grofield thought at first she was leading him directly from the back of the house into the jungle.

But it wasn't jungle. It wasn't even the back of the house, but a central courtyard around which the house made an enclosed square, the courtyard about twenty feet on a side. Jungle growth was so thick here that the rear of the house couldn't be seen through it, and the meandering slate path that Belle Danamato now set off on was visible for only a few steps.

Grofield followed her in, vines and leaves brushing his shoulders. The sun's heat was lessened in here, but not all the way down to the clamminess in the jungle proper.

In the middle of this pocket jungle was a tiny clearing, barely four feet square, paved with irregular-shaped pieces of slate and containing a glass-topped wrought-iron table and four delicate-looking wrought-iron chairs. Belle Danamato motioned for Grofield to sit down, took the chair opposite him, and reached out behind her to press an inconspicuous button on a tree.

By now Grofield was prepared to be unsurprised by anything. If the button pushing had resulted in the whole clearing suddenly sinking into the bowels of the earth—or, conversely, taking off like a flying saucer—he would merely have nodded. But there was no visible result at all, though there was a clue to the button's function in what she next said to him:

"I hope you like rum."

"Love rum," Grofield said.

"Good. As long as we're in Puerto Rico there's no point drinking anything else."

"You aren't a native," Grofield suggested.

She smiled and reached out briefly to pat his hand, saying, "We'll get to it, Mr. Grofield. I'm sure you had a harrowing drive."

"Route three will never be my favorite."

"I sometimes wonder where they're all going."

Grofield said, "You've lived here long?"

"Don't rush me," she said, and this time there was no smile, no pat of the hand. A little of the steel showed through, a little of the impatience of a woman used to money, used to service, used to not getting an argument.

Grofield shook his head. "I'm sorry, Mrs. Danamato," he said. "I don't know what you want from me, but I don't think I'm exactly what you have in mind. Some employment service might be able to find someone suitable for you." He got to his feet.

She looked up at him in surprise. "My God. Are you really that touchy?"

"I'm independently wealthy," he told her, which was very nearly true, at least at the moment. He'd barely begun to spend the proceeds of his last job; it would be another year or more before he'd have to start looking for another one. And then it wouldn't involve pulling the forelock for Belle Danamato or anybody else.

Now she was saying, "I understood you were a free-lance, you might be—"

"A free-lance what?"

She made an irritated shrug. "How do I know? Adventurer, soldier of fortune, call it what you want."

"You call it. It's wrong. Goodbye, Mrs. Danamato."

He turned and almost collided with a stout woman in a floral-pattern dress who was carrying a tray with two drinks on it. They did a dance of a step or two, disaster was averted, and Grofield headed back toward the French doors.

Behind him Belle Danamato called, "At least have a drink!" Then, when he kept going: "Aren't you even curious?"

That deserved a response. He turned where he was on the path, midway between table and house, where he was already looking back at her through greenery, as though the two of them were extras in a tropical production of *Alice in Wonderland.* "I'm very curious," he said. The stout woman was standing where he'd left her, looking in bewilderment back and forth at the two of them. "I'm sorry," Grofield went on, "that I'll never know what all this was about. But I was met by a dog and a shotgun, I was searched and got a barely passing grade because I didn't have a gun on me, and now you want to play croquet for an hour before letting me know what's up. I don't like the set-up. It smells as though you want to hire a hood to play servant, and I'm neither. Goodbye, Mrs. Danamato."

She called something else, but he didn't hear it. He went through the French doors, through the house, down the driveway to the Ford. No one came after him, no one appeared anywhere, though he half expected the German shepherd suddenly to round a corner and have at his throat.

The inside of the Ford was baking hot, the windowsill too hot to touch. Grofield's suitcase on the back seat appeared to have been left untouched, though it hardly mattered, since there was nothing in it anyway but clothing and toilet articles.

Grofield started the Ford, drove it around the circular drive and back into the dim trail down through the jungle. The interior of the car cooled off at once, and where Grofield had perspired his shirt was now cold and wet against his skin.

He came down to the dirt road, turned left, drove the four-tenths of a mile back to route 185. He stopped at the intersection, and the passenger door opened. Out of nowhere a smiling bearded man, barefoot and in filthy once-white trousers and once-white shirt, a blue-black Colt .45 automatic huge in his hand, slid in and shut the door. His smile showed clean and perfect teeth. He said, "Turn right, you great big hunk of man."

"No riders," Grofield said. "Didn't you see the sign?"

The smile didn't change an ounce. "Don't cause me trouble, honey," he said. "They make me buy my own bullets."

Grofield looked at him, saw that behind the smiling mouth and the mock-cute speech the eyes were cold and the Colt was off safety, and decided that if this bird had wanted to kill him he didn't have to get into the car to do it. Grofield nodded. "The customer's always right."

"Beautiful *and* smart," said the bearded man.

Grofield turned right, south, away from Toma de Agua, away from Loiza and the airport and everything else.

3

"TURN right, green eyes."

Grofield tapped the brake and looked at the unbroken line of jungle growth on the right. "There doesn't seem to be any road," he said.

"Right in there, sweetness."

The bearded man had pointed toward an area that looked just as dense as the rest of it. Shrugging, Grofield spun the wheel to the right and moved gingerly forward into the greenery.

It parted before his hood, leaves and vines and hanging shrubs sliding aside to let the car in. For one second the windshield was blotted entirely by the purplish-white, flat underbellies of leaves, the interior of the car got green dark, and Grofield considered something foolish like sudden acceleration or sudden braking combined with a grab for the gun; but then the leaves parted, the foolish second was over, and the car was a scant few yards from a rundown wooden shack that had at one time been painted a really gaudy blue, with pink trim. Only here and there now could those colors be seen through the pervasive gray of age.

The packed earth area between the shack and the hedge of jungle growth along the roadside was crammed with empty chicken crates, rusted automobile parts, bent and blistered metal beer signs, decaying wooden chairs and all manner of general junk, leaving just barely enough room for the Ford. In fact, before Grofield hit the brake his front bumper hit an oil drum and knocked it over with a clang.

"Sloppy," commented the bearded man.

"Let me go back to the airport and run the whole thing again."

"Ho ho," said the bearded man, deadpan. He reached out, cut the ignition, and took the key. "You get outsville, love."

"Anything your gun says."

Grofield got out, leaving the door open. The bearded man slid over behind the wheel and said, "Get in front of the car, dumplin. That's the way I want to remember you, always."

Grofield shrugged and went around in front of the car. He noticed that the oil drum had been dented but the Ford's bumper was unmarked. The rental agency would be happy about that, if they ever saw the car again.

The bearded man had restarted the engine. Grofield, braced to jump to the side if it was the bearded man's intention to run him down, almost lost his balance from being too ready in the wrong direction when what the bearded man did was back the car instead. It slipped through the greenery with a slishing sound and was gone.

Grofield stood there and didn't believe it. Was the whole thing nothing but a car heist? And why hadn't the Ford been creamed by a passing car when it had suddenly backed into the roadway from—apparently—nowhere?

Well, that part was easy. That road out there looked about as well-traveled as Death Valley, though hardly for the same reason. They were deeply in the jungle now, on a dirt road off a gravel road off a blacktop road, eighteen twisting up-and-down miles from where the bearded man had joined the party. None of the roads had been marked, so Grofield had no idea now where he was or even in what direction to find San Juan.

But why go through all this simply to steal the car? A thousand other places along the road would have served just as well for dumping Grofield, if that was all it was.

Grofield looked around, trying to figure out why this spot and no other. It was just an empty shack and a littered yard, screened from the road, with nothing remarkable about it.

So what now? Should he go over to the shack, or should he leave? There might be something in there to explain what this was all about, but on the other hand he might be better off getting out of this neighborhood before something else happened.

He didn't get a chance to make up his mind, because something else happened right away. As he stood there, looking this way and that, trying to make up his mind, another car suddenly jolted through the greenery, filling up the space where the Ford had been, barely missing Grofield and coming to a stop inches from the overturned oil drum.

It was a Mercedes, black, highly polished, its chrome reflecting distorted Grofields against a background of white. The two rear doors opened and two men got out, both in severely cut dark suits and narrow dark ties. The one on Grofield's right unshucked a small revolver from a shoulder holster and held it with his hand and arm resting casually on the top of the car. The other one came walking forward, stepping with care, making grimaces at the litter all over the place. Both of them were about thirty, medium height, slender, with narrow, tight faces.

Grofield rested one hand on the Mercedes hood, feeling it very hot under his fingers, which probably meant the car had come a considerable distance. More than likely from San Juan.

Well. This shouldn't be difficult. All he had to contend with were these two. Plus, of course, the driver, anonymous behind the glare of the windshield, nothing clearly visible but his hands high on the wheel.

That was all. Three men, at least one armed. Nothing to it. All Grofield had to do was stand where he was and wait to see what these people intended to do with him.

The one who'd come walking forward stopped just out of arm's reach, put out his hand and said, "Your wallet."

"This," Grofield said, "is the most stylish mugging I've ever been a party to." He reached into his hip pocket, took out his wallet slowly enough for the one with the gun to see it was really a wallet, and handed it over to the one who talked.

The other took it from him, opened it, riffled through the plastic pockets containing Grofield's cards, stopped at one to study it, and then turned the wallet around so Grofield could see it, too. He said, "What's that?"

Grofield looked. "Equity card," he said.

"Explain."

Grofield spread his hands. "What's to explain? I'm an actor, Actors Equity is my union, that's my union card."

The talker frowned at the card. It seemed to trouble him the way Grofield's lack of a gun had troubled Mrs. Danamato's garrison. Finally he shook his head, reached inside his suit jacket, and took out a thing that looked like a tan pencil flashlight, with a tan plastic cord attached to it that ran back down inside the jacket. Holding the end of this thing near his mouth and speaking softly, he said, "Alan Grofield. Ohio driver's license, number Z437 dash 52689 dash 881. Claims to be an actor, has a card in the same name from Actors Equity, a union. Social Security card, number 059 space 26 space 0281. Three addresses on three different forms, one Marion, Ohio, one New York City, one Santa Barbara, California. Two hundred twenty-seven dollars American bills. Other cards and forms, none significant."

Grofield watched him with growing amazement. Was he really committing all that stuff to a pocket tape recorder?

There was a button on the side of the microphone which the other had held down with his thumb while speaking. Now he released it, closed Grofield's wallet again, and tossed it back to him. Grofield caught it and said, "Thank you. May I put it away?"

"Yes."

"Thanks again. You're too kind."

The other depressed the button, held the microphone near his mouth, and said, "Why did you go to see Mrs. Danamato?" Then he extended the microphone toward Grofield.

Grofield smiled at the microphone. "None of your business," he told it politely.

The other shook his head, released the button, and said, "Don't waste everybody's time. Just answer the questions."

The bureaucratic boredom of the bastard, his weary confidence, his calm acceptance of the idea that Grofield wouldn't do anything but cooperate, it was all infuriating. Grofield said, "Don't waste your time? What about my time? How often do you think I get to vacation in Puerto Rico? What about my car? Do you realize it's costing me eleven cents a mile for that weirdo friend of yours to take it for a joy ride?"

"Mrs. Danamato rented that automobile," the other said, "using the name Wilcox, the same name you used when you picked it up. It is now being returned to the rental agency. Why make things difficult for yourself? Just answer the questions and we can all go about our business. Why did you go see Mrs. Danamato?" He held out the microphone again, button depressed.

"To get laid," Grofield said.

Surprisingly, a sudden flush reddened the other's face, and he yanked the microphone back as though Grofield had tried to bite it. "Watch that crap!" he said angrily, pitching his voice low and urgent, as though afraid of being overheard.

"Stop trying to impress me," Grofield told him.

The one with the revolver said, in a peevish voice, "Whyn't we just bump him? Then it don't matter why he went there."

Some people said things like that, and it was a bluff meant to throw a scare into somebody. Other people said things like that, and they meant it. Grofield looked at this one, and he thought he was the kind who meant it.

But the one with the microphone shook his head. "B.G. wants a report," he said.

The other one said, "But what if this one won't give us a report?"

"I've got nothing to give," Grofield told them.

The questioner stuck the microphone toward him, saying irritably, "Into the mike."

"Nothing to report," Grofield said into the mike. "I'm not refusing to answer, I just don't have any answers."

"Crapola," said the one with the revolver.

The other one, holding the mike close, said, "You got to know why you went there."

"A man in South America paid my airline tickets to come here," Grofield said. "He didn't say why, or who I was going to see, or what it was about."

"Who was this man?"

"You want me to tell my story or not?"

The questioner shrugged. "All right," he said. "We'll come back to it."

"We won't. I came here, I followed directions, I met Mrs. Danamato. We didn't get along, she thought I was a butler or something, I walked out before she got around to telling me what she wanted. I drove away and got snatched. End of story."

"Who was the man in South America?"

"I suppose he's a friend of Mrs. Danamato's."

"What's his name?"

"What's yours?" Grofield said.

The questioner pulled the microphone back and released the button. He studied Grofield somberly for a minute and then nodded, as though having come to a decision. "You will leave Puerto Rico," he said. "On the first available flight. You will keep your nose out of other people's business."

"What about my car?"

"It will be returned to the rental agency."

The questioner turned away, went back to the rear door of the car.

Grofield said, "How do I get back to San Juan?"

Nobody answered him. The questioner got into the Mercedes and then the other one got in on the other side. The car backed up, slid through the screen of leaves, disappeared.

Grofield stood where he was. "Son of a bitch," he said.

4

THE house looked pink in the sunset, with orange eyes. No white-garbed men appeared, with or without dogs. Grofield moved across the lawn, keeping to the edge of the jungle, and approached the house at last from the rear.

It had taken him almost three hours to work his way back here, walking and hitchhiking. The least Belle Danamato owed him was an explanation and a ride back to town, and maybe she also owed him hotel accommodations and plane fare to New York. It depended on how irritated he was with her when she was done telling him what was going on. At the moment he was about irritated enough to burn her house down and kick her in the head when she came running out.

There were various lit windows here and there around the house, these yellow instead of the orange sun reflection of the others, but the first-floor windows in the area where Grofield approached were all dark. They included two sets of French doors, toward which Grofield hurried. The first knob he tried turned easily and the door pulled open with a flutter of thin curtain. Grofield stepped through into darkness and shut the door behind him.

After a minute he could make out vague masses of furniture and across the way a doorway leading to an area somewhat more lighted. He made his way cautiously through the room to that doorway, found himself in a corridor with light down to the left, and moved that way.

The corridor emptied onto that central courtyard where he'd not quite had a drink. Just before it, a sitting room on the right was well lighted but empty. Grofield went through there, opened the door on the other side, and a short, heavy-set guy with cauliflower ears and a mashed nose held a Colt .45 automatic where Grofield could see it glint in the light. "Back up," said the guy, and Grofield backed up.

The guy followed him into the room. He was very nicely turned out, with a black suit, white shirt, dark figured necktie, polished black shoes, but above all the sartorial splendor was the bread-dough face of a sparring partner.

The bread-dough face opened its mouth and said, "Turn around."

Grofield turned around. Hands patted him and he said, "I don't have a gun this time either."

"Shut up."

Grofield shut up. He could hear a loud wheezing sound, which was the guy drawing air in through that broken nose.

The hands stopped patting after a while, and the guy said, "Start walking. Out that door, and left down the corridor."

Grofield walked. He retraced his steps down the corridor, but continued on past the room he'd started from, and at the other end of the corridor he was directed to turn left, go through another small sitting room, and then enter a formal dining room where six people were seated at table. Belle Danamato was at the head.

Grofield said, "Hello again."

Everybody looked up. Belle Danamato said, "Where'd *you* come from?"

The guy behind Grofield said, "I found him pussyfooting around."

Grofield said, "Mrs. Danamato, tell your man to put his gun away."

Belle Danamato didn't seem very friendly. She said, "Why should I?"

Grofield spun on his right heel, knocking the automatic to one side with his left elbow while driving his right forearm into the guy's throat. The automatic made a soft thump when it hit the rug; the guy made a big thump when he hit the wall and started his slide down, both hands grabbing his neck.

Grofield picked up the automatic, turned around with it, pointed it at Belle Danamato and said, "Ask me not to shoot."

One of the men at the table said, "Now see here," and started up from his chair.

Grofield pointed the automatic at him. "Don't make me lose my temper," he said.

Belle Danamato said, "Sit down, George."

George sat down.

Grofield pointed the automatic at her again. "Ask me not to shoot," he said.

"Why?"

"Because if you don't, I will."

She was unruffled, but she did frown with interest. "Why?" she said.

"Because when I left here I was strong-armed and humiliated and my car was stolen. And you're responsible."

One of the other women at the table said, "It's Ben!"

"Of course," Belle Danamato said, not looking away from Grofield. "You're right," she said to Grofield. "I did cause your trouble, though I swear I didn't know it would happen. I apologize, and I ask you not to shoot me."

"Done," said Grofield. He pulled the clip out of the handle, tossed the automatic on the table, flipped the clip onto the floor in a corner of the room. "Now tell me the story," he said.

The guy who'd started to get up before, the one she'd called George, now said, "This isn't the way to do it. Belle, may I?"

She shrugged. "Go ahead."

George got to his feet. He was medium height, about forty,

very thin hair, round eyeglasses, rumpled brown suit and tie, dandruff on the shoulders. He said, "We'll talk in another room, Mr.—?"

Belle Danamato said, "His name's Alan Grofield."

"Mr. Grofield," said George. "I am George Milford, Mrs. Danamato's attorney. Shall we go?"

"Lead the way," said Grofield. He turned, and the sparring partner was still sitting on the floor, now holding his neck with only one hand. He looked up at Grofield and said, "I am never going to like you." His voice was raspier than before.

"That'll be a loss in my life," Grofield told him.

George Milford led the way out of the dining room and through a few other rooms, turning on lights along the way, till he came to a kind of library or den. There were two black leather chairs facing each other, with a large round coffee table between, with inlaid tile mosaic. "Sit down," Milford said. "Care for a drink?"

"Gin and tonic."

There was a well-stocked bar in one area of the bookcase, with its own ice-maker. Milford made drinks, gave Grofield his, sat down in the other leather chair and said, "I can understand your annoyance. I'll tell you anything you want to know, but before I do would you mind telling me what happened after you left here this afternoon?"

Grofield told him, briefly. Milford wanted descriptions of the men involved, but whether the descriptions rang any bell for him or not Grofield couldn't tell.

When Grofield was done, Milford said, "I take it Mrs. Danamato's name means nothing to you?"

"Not before today."

"Then you've never heard of B.G. Danamato either. Benjamin Danamato."

"B.G. was who those guys were going to report to," Grofield said. "Would that be the same one?"

"It would," Milford said. "He's Belle's husband."

Grofield made a face. "I'm involved with a jealous husband?"

"Not exactly," Milford said. "B.G. isn't jealous, not in the usual sense. It might help if I tell you he's a mobster. He operates big-time gambling structures in the States."

"It tells me where he got those friends from," Grofield said. "Otherwise, it doesn't help. It doesn't tell me what Mrs. Danamato wanted to hire me for, and it doesn't tell me why her husband's people tried to intimidate me."

Milford said, "Of course." Then he sank into a brown study, rubbing his chin with the fingers of one hand, brooding, his eyes on Grofield as though Grofield was a painting which just might be a clever forgery.

Grofield let him go on for half a minute, then said, "You're her lawyer, right?"

"Yes, I am."

"Then right now you're doing what lawyers do," Grofield told him.

Milford seemed somewhat surprised. "I am? What's that?"

"You're trying to decide how little you can tell me, without actually lying, and both satisfy my desire to know and your desire to maintain security."

Milford made a small and crooked smile. "I suppose I was," he said. "One does tend to think in terms of secrecy after a while, in a matter like this."

"A matter like what?"

Milford nodded. "All right. You have been treated shabbily, and you do deserve to know. The fact of the matter is, Mrs. Danamato is in the process of divorcing her husband."

"Contested?"

"Not exactly," Milford said. "The settlement is quite complicated, that's all. Both parties are agreeable to the action, but the details are taking some ironing out."

"Are they?"

"In the meantime," Milford said, "Mrs. Danamato believes her life may be in jeopardy. I'm not prepared to state whether or not her belief is justified."

"I didn't think you would be," Grofield said.

"Whether or not she is justified," Milford said, "she has taken precautions. Harry is one."

"Harry?"

"The man you took the gun away from. He is her personal bodyguard."

Grofield grinned. "Then I'm glad I'm not her insurance man," he said.

"Harry is better than he appeared in the dining room," Milford said. "You seemed to be engaging in civilized discourse with Belle. There was no reason for Harry to suppose you were suddenly going to turn violent."

"If Harry's a bodyguard," Grofield said, "he's supposed to suppose everybody will turn violent."

Milford's smile was thin. "Granted," he said.

Grofield said, "I guess those two Pancho Villas with the dog are more precautions."

"Yes. They guard the grounds."

"Where were they when I came in just now?"

"Eating, I assume."

"Both of them?"

Milford smiled again, just as thinly. "You seem to have established a number of weaknesses in Belle's defenses."

"Happy to oblige," said Grofield. "Now, let's get to me. What was supposed to be my part in the plot?"

"You've seen Harry," Milford said. "Whatever his abilities or deficiencies as a bodyguard, you must admit he would not be considered the ideal escort for an attractive woman in a public place."

"Except maybe Madison Square Garden."

"Exactly. What Belle wanted was someone to take Harry's place in public. Someone who could fulfill Harry's function of bodyguard and yet be acceptable in appearance."

"That's flattering," Grofield said. "How'd it happen to be me?"

"Our normal sources for such an employee," Milford said carefully, "were unfortunately closed to us."

"Why?"

Milford spread his hands. "We would never be sure the man wasn't more loyal to Belle's husband than to Belle."

There was a knock at the door. Milford turned his head, calling, "Come in."

It was Belle Danamato. She said, "You done?"

"Just about," Milford said. He looked at Grofield. "Unless you have more questions."

Grofield said, "I take it B.G. is keeping an eye on this place. They saw me go in . . . No, they knew I was coming, knew about the Wilcox name at the airport. But they didn't know what I was supposed to be for. So when I came out, they asked me."

"Yes."

"Wonderful," said Grofield.

Belle Danamato said to Grofield, "Did George tell you what I wanted to hire you for?"

"Yes."

"The job is still available," she said.

"I'm still not," Grofield told her.

"Why not?"

"It's not my line of work, in the first place," Grofield said. "And in the second place, if I was going to be somebody's bodyguard, I'd have to like the person I was guarding. Otherwise I might tend to be sloppy."

Belle Danamato flushed. "And you don't like me?"

"Not even a little bit," Grofield said.

Milford, politely shocked, murmured, "Please, Mr. Grofield."

"Let him alone," Belle Danamato said. To Grofield she said, "What's the problem? Why are you so down on me?"

"You're arrogant," Grofield said. "Without reason. At your age a woman shouldn't be a spoiled brat."

"You *are* a bastard," she said coldly. "I'd had a place set for you at the table, but I think you'd prefer to leave at once."

"On the contrary," Grofield said. "I haven't eaten since lunch on the plane. Dinner's a good idea." He got to his feet, said to Milford, "You coming?"

5

THE extra place was set at the foot of the table. Sitting there, Grofield was facing Belle Danamato, angry and tight-lipped, at the head, with the six others grouped three on each side.

Grofield smiled at them all and said, "Mrs. Danamato forgot to introduce me. My name is Alan Grofield. I was invited here."

"In error," snapped Belle Danamato.

George Milford was sitting to her left, and he now took her hand in his own, saying softly, "Take it easy, Belle."

Harry the bodyguard was to Grofield's immediate right. Grofield smiled at him and said, "Let's see. I know you."

"I know you, too, buddy," Harry said grimly. His voice was still a little hoarse.

Grofield ignored that, looking instead at the woman past Harry, between Harry and George Milford. She was a severely girdled middle-aged woman in a dark suit too heavy for the climate, her mouth down-turned in what seemed to be a permanent expression of disapproval. Her hair was in a permanent so tight and rigid it looked as though it had to be painful.

Grofield gave this personage his most charming smile, saying, "But this lovely lady and I haven't met."

"My wife," George Milford said sourly. Then, with an obvious effort to be more polite, he said, "Eva, this is Mr. Grofield."

"Alan," said Grofield.

She nodded at him, her eyes flicking in his direction and then away again as her lips moved and something small and birdlike was murmured between them. Grofield understood that the severity of her appearance was a form of protection, that she was painfully shy and self-conscious. Not wanting to be sadistic to her, he merely nodded back, smiled amiably, and switched his attention to the man nearest on his left.

This one was different. An African apparently, in robes of maroon and white, with a sort of maroon pillbox on his head. His skin was extremely dark, almost totally black, with no brown pigmentation at all. His face was impassive, ageless. He returned Grofield's look with an absolutely blank look of his own.

Grofield met his gaze for a few seconds, then smiled again and said, "Alan Grofield."

Was that a smile on the other's face? If so, it was too slight to matter. His voice was soft, almost as semiexistent as the smile, as he answered, "How do you do? I am Onum Marba." His accent was slight but unmistakable and seemed to imply that his native tongue tended heavily to clicks.

"Mr. Marba," Grofield said, and nodded his head in a tiny bow, then moved his gaze to Marba's left.

Now here was the winner of the evening. If this was the body to be guarded, Grofield wouldn't hesitate for a second. A lovely girl of twenty-something, as slender as a spring evening, she had long ash-blond hair and a level brown-eyed gaze. Her manner, as she studied Grofield, not so much meeting his eyes as looking past them into his head, was solemn, thoughtful, as a doe might look at the first hunter of autumn.

Grofield's smile as he gazed at the winner was perhaps broader than it had been before. "And good evening to *you*," he said.

Her one flaw seemed to be a lack of humor. Grofield hoped not; he preferred to think her sense of humor was being held in check for this reason or that.

In any case, her expression remained solemn as she said, "Good evening. I'm Patricia Chelm."

"Good evening, Patricia Chelm."

She looked away from him to gesture to the young man on her left, saying, "And this is my brother, Roy."

Roy Chelm was as slender as his sister, but on a male it didn't look quite so good. His faee was weaker than his sister's, too, even a bit petulant. He looked away from the introduction and said to Belle Danamato, "Belle, do we really need him here? I mean, after all."

"It doesn't matter," she said as the heavy-set woman servant Grofield had seen earlier today came in with a tray bearing bowls of soup. "He isn't staying. He won't take the job."

"Good," said Roy Chelm. His voice had weakness in it, too.

A bowl of soup was placed in front of Grofield. "I hate to eat and run," he said, picking up his spoon, "but I'll be leaving right after dinner."

"Tomorrow," said Milford.

Grofield looked up.

Milford said, "You'll never get a plane out tonight, Grofield. Nor a hotel room, without a reservation. You can stay here tonight, and I'll drive you to the airport in the morning."

"All right," Grofield said. He tried the soup. Vichysoisse. Excellent for a hot night.

6

THE scream brought him out of bed on the run.

Grofield's two professions often complemented each other, the training in one reinforcing the training in the other, and between acting and thievery his reaction time to the unexpected had become very fast indeed. Before the last echoes of the scream had died away, he was on his feet, in his pants, and headed for the door.

God alone knew what time it was. He'd come up to his room around eleven, not so much because he was tired as because the company downstairs was so painfully dull. The African, Marba, sat around watching everybody like a cat on a hearth. Belle Danamato carried her arrogance and bad temper around like a merit badge, with Roy Chelm in constant Uriah Heep attendance on her. Could Chelm be anything but a gigolo, the other private half of what Grofield was to have been for her in public? He could see that Harry and Chelm between them served at home in the capacity she had wanted to hire him for in her public appearances, and he wasn't sure whether he should be complimented or disgusted.

In any case, Chelm's sister had obviously inherited all the guts in the family. If she'd only inherited some sense of humor as well. But if Marba sat around like a cat, Patricia Chelm sat around like a solemn faun, silent and unapproachable, lovely but no fun.

As for the Milfords, they weren't much fun either. The husband was the only one present trying for any kind of normal polite civilized discourse, and his attempts were more painful than silence. But when there was silence, his desperately shy and self-conscious wife filled it with her own painful silence the way an aching tooth fills a head.

Grofield stuck it out as long as he could, but even an unending string of daiquiris on the rocks didn't help, and he finally left the living room where the torture was taking place, wandered around till he found a library, scanned it, settled reluctantly for a novel by Lloyd Douglas, and went upstairs to his room.

He had no suitcase now. With any luck he'd be able to pick it up from the car-rental agency tomorrow. In the meantime, he had to brush his teeth with his finger and borrowed toothpaste, after which Lloyd Douglas put him peacefully to sleep for X hours and X minutes, ending with the scream.

Grofield's room was dark, but the corridor was lighted. He yanked open his door, squinted in the light for a few seconds, looked to the left, looked to the right, and saw Patricia Chelm backing out of a room on the other side of the hall. The back of her hand was to her mouth, and she was staring in frozen shock at something inside the room.

Grofield hurried down there, put his hand on her shoulder, said, "What is it?"

She didn't react, neither to his hand nor to his voice. He sensed doors opening up and down the hall. He turned and looked into the room she'd come backing out of, and Belle Danamato was lying on the floor in there beside the bed, fully dressed, staring pop-eyed at the ceiling. Her face was purple.

Grofield stepped into the room, saw the wire around her neck, knew she wasn't breathing, and turned around to see Harry in the doorway, wearing yellow pajamas with race horses all over them and holding in his right hand the same old Colt automatic.

"Hands on your head, bo," said Harry. Behind him, Roy Chelm had appeared and was standing there with his arms around his sister, whose head was buried against his shoulder.

"She's dead," Grofield said. "Garrotted."

"I said hands on your head," said Harry. "I'd be happy to plug you."

"You know I didn't do this," Grofield told him, but he didn't like Harry's expression, so he put his hands on top of his head.

"You and nobody else," Harry said. "Turn around."

Grofield turned around. Harry frisked him from behind, and Grofield said, "I'm just as clean as I was the last time."

"Shut up."

Grofield shrugged and waited it out.

George Milford came into the room and into Grofield's line of vision. He looked down at Belle Danamato, shook his head grimly, and said, "What a mess."

Harry was done. "Okay, bo," he said. "Turn around and walk outa here."

Milford said to Harry. "It was him?"

"Who else?" Harry said.

"Somebody else," Grofield said.

Milford looked at Grofield heavily. "So B.G.'s people got to you," he said. "We knew you were for sale to the highest bidder, but you should have at least given us a chance to put in our bid."

Grofield shook his head. "You're wrong, Milford," he said.

Milford looked past him at Harry. "What are you going to do with him?"

"Lock him away till the law gets here," Harry said. "Only he didn't do this for B.G., he did it on his own hook."

"How do you know that?" Milford asked him.

"Because I'm working for B.G.," Harry said calmly. "If he wanted Mrs. Danamato dead, he would've told me."

Grofield said to Milford, "You see this doesn't make any sense, don't you?"

"No, I don't. Where will you put him, Harry?" It didn't seem to surprise or bother Milford to learn that Harry was actually working for the husband.

"There's a storeroom in the cellar," Harry said.

"Can I bring my book along?" Grofield asked. "I was just to the exciting part."

"Move, bo," said Harry.

7

THE room was gray, windowless, about ten feet square and with a ceiling of barely seven feet. Rough wooden shelves ringed the rough cement walls, and the rough wooden door looked about as heavy as a young elephant. The shelves were empty and so was the room.

Grofield was barefoot, and the concrete floor was cold, so he tended to stand in one place. He was wearing trousers and T-shirt, which weren't enough for this chilly and slightly clammy room. There was one dim light bulb in the ceiling, which Grofield had left on even though there wasn't much of anything to see.

Or do. Harry hadn't given him another shot at the automatic, though all the way down here to this basement storeroom Grofield had been looking for a chance to get on top of the situation. Well. The situation was on top of him, and the prospects were gloomy.

Grofield was depressed. Standing there on the cold floor, on that one little patch of it slightly warmed by his feet, his arms wrapped around himself for whatever warmth that might give, surrounded by emptiness and dim light, he felt very very sorry for himself.

He knew the feeling was at least partly irrational, the result of physical discomfort. Keeping their victims chilly and underfed and underslept had long been one of the most potent weapons of the brainwashers, inducing depression and self-pity and eventually despair. But though he might be cold and uncomfortable, he was hardly underfed, and if he was underslept in the short run his body was definitely resilient enough to take an interrupted night's sleep in stride.

No, it was the clamminess. Plus, of course, the inaction, the inability to do anything or think constructively about anything or plan anything. And also there was the undeniable extra little problem that he might be shot very soon.

They were waiting for the employees of Belle Danamato's husband. Harry was one of them himself and apparently had a way to contact the others. And what would he tell them on arrival? "The boss's wife is dead, and I got the killer in the cellar."

Wonderful.

And what would the reaction of the others be? Well, they would probably get in touch with B.G. Danamato himself first and tell him the situation. And B.G. would surely answer, "Execute."

Magnificent.

It was rare for Grofield to be the innocent bystander, and he didn't much like it. When he was guilty, as he frequently was, he was exclusively guilty of well-planned and well-executed major robberies with a cast of perhaps five or six, where most of the details and most of the potential results were already counted on within the plan. If the plan were to go sour—as sometimes even the best-laid plans did—it would nevertheless do so within a perimeter of the known. Grofield would know how to act. More important, he would know how to react.

But here he was in the middle of somebody else's story. To take a simile from his second profession, he had been miscast.

Not only that, he'd been thrust onstage without knowing his lines.

All right. If that door over there should ever open, Grofield was prepared to ad-lib with the best of them, hoping for the best. In the meantime, there was nothing to do but stand here and shiver and be gloomy and depressed and sorry for himself and bored.

No. Come to think of it, there was one other thing he could do. He could go over the story till now, he could try to familiarize himself with the material, so that when the door finally did open—assuming they didn't merely intend to leave him down here forever, à la "Cask of Amontillado"—his ad libs would have some weight and point.

For instance. George Milford had told him something of the situation here, but had he told all? Hardly. There were holes in his story you could drive a 747 through. So, go over what Milford had said and see if anything could be figured out about what Milford hadn't said.

Milford had said: Belle Danamato was separated from her husband, getting a divorce from him. She was afraid he was going to kill her. The divorce was uncontested, but the settlement was complicated. She had Harry for her bodyguard at home, but he wouldn't do for public appearances, so she was looking for someone to escort her in the outside world.

Fine. Question: If the divorce was uncontested and the settlement—though complicated—was at least in the process of being settled, why was Belle Danamato afraid her husband was going to kill her? Answer: Milford was lying. Either the divorce *was* contested, or the settlement was too complicated to be worked out. Of the two, Grofield leaned toward the second, on the theory that a man doesn't kill his wife to keep her from leaving him. It would be the settlement. Money.

Grofield smiled, in the small cold room, under the small dim light. He smiled because he was pleased with himself, and he was pleased with himself because he'd worked it out. If husband Danamato was a big-time racketeer, as claimed, he undoubtedly had income-tax problems. If he had income-tax problems, he undoubtedly had an accountant. And if he had an accountant—

and listened to the accountant—a lot of his holdings were undoubtedly in his wife's name.

Sure. She could divorce him if she wanted, but he was
damned if she'd walk away with half his goods. So then the
situation became obvious: He must have let her know that she
would either sign all that stuff back over to him or he'd arrange
to inherit from her.

So down came Belle Danamato to Puerto Rico, with her
lawyer and a few friends, prepared to lock herself out of sight
until her husband gave up or the divorce proceedings became
final.

So had B.G. Danamato made good on his threat? Had his
wife been right in her fears, and had he gotten to her despite
her precautions?

No. Not if Harry was actually working for the husband, as
he'd said he was. Belle Danamato could have been killed at any
time. No reason to wait until now.

Unless . . .

Grofield stopped smiling and hugged himself tighter. Unless,
he thought, they didn't want to make a move until a patsy
showed up.

Would that make sense? A man can't legally inherit as a result
of a felony he committed. If Belle Danamato were murdered
there'd be no suspect around but her husband, or at least one of
her husband's employees. The police would surely do their best
to shake up Danamato's organization until a stool pigeon fell
out, and a man can never be sure that every last one of his
employees is 100 per cent trustworthy and true. Not with a lot
of police pressure on them.

But what if there's another murderer, a wanderer, a drifter,
just drifted in, had an argument with Mrs. Danamato, actually
threatened her with a gun at the dinner table? Why should the
law look any farther, why should there be any shake-up of
Danamato's organization?

Was George Milford in on it? He hadn't acted surprised when
Harry told him his true affiliation, but on the other hand Harry
had apparently felt the need to tell him. So Milford hadn't
actually known that Harry was in the house really as the

husband's employee, but he had suspected it. Confirmation had come as no surprise.

Whose side was Milford on? If he'd suspected Harry to be disloyal, why hadn't he told Mrs. Danamato? Or was he maintaining an Olympian dispassion, a grand neutrality, planning to ride the coattails of whoever came out on top?

And what about the others? Roy Chelm was obviously what Belle Danamato was getting her divorce for, and his sister Patricia was either here on vacation or to protect her from any overflow revenge of B.G.'s. The same for Milford's wife, the tense Eva. As to Onum Marba, the poker-faced African, his role in all this was pure bafflement.

Another question finally occurred to Grofield. Assuming he was wrong about Harry having done the killing—an assumption he would be delighted to make—who else was likely? The brother and sister Chelm seemed both to be in a position to gain a lot more from keeping Belle Danamato alive. George Milford didn't seem to have any motive for switching from observer to participant, and neither did his wife. Onum Marba? First you'd have to know what he was there for. Still, poker faces are usually worn by poker players, so whatever he was doing here it was unlikely Marba included murder on the agenda.

Which left Harry, damn it. Good old Harry.

Speak of the devil. The door creaked open, and there was Harry in the doorway, automatic in hand. This time he had two friends with him, one the pistol packer from the Mercedes, the other a new face. They both had guns in their hands, too.

What did they think he was—Rasputin?

"Come on, bo," said Harry. "Let's take a walk."

8

THE sun was up. Amazing. How many hours had he shivered down there, for Pete's sake?

In any case, the sun was a welcome warmth on his face when he walked out of the house, following Harry, the other two behind him, and the sun-warmed flagstones were heaven on his feet.

This was the central courtyard again, the pocket jungle. They'd brought him upstairs and through a confusing series of rooms and out a set of French doors, and here was the court. Harry set off toward the middle of it on the curving flagstone path.

What were they going to do, murder him and bury the body in the middle of the court?

Nonsense. They wanted him around to show to the law, to be accused of murder, to take the rap for B.G. and his boys.

Nevertheless, Grofield hesitated just a second before following Harry. A gun was immediately poked into his back, and a voice said, "Move along, chum."

He moved along.

Once again there was that brief instant when the jungle growth was all that could be seen in any direction, when the house ceased to exist and the mind began to jitter with the irrational shakes, but one step more and there was the clearing, slate-floored, with its table and chairs.

And B.G. Danamato.

It couldn't be anybody else. A big heavy-set man, dressed in a lightweight business suit and sprawled broadly on one of the flimsy ice-cream chairs, he was puffing away on a cigar as though to illustrate his contempt of clichés. As Grofield approached, Danamato took the cigar from his mouth and studied him like a slave auctioneer appraising the day's goods.

Grofield came to a stop on the other side of the table. "Lee J. Cobb, I presume," he said.

"Danamato," corrected Danamato. "B.G. Danamato."

"Grofield," Grofield said. "A.J. Grofield."

Danamato pointed his cigar. "Sit down."

Grofield sat down. "Are we having breakfast?" By the slant of the sun, he assumed it was around nine in the morning.

"Don't worry about breakfast," Danamato told him. "You won't be alive long enough to miss it."

"That's a relief," said Grofield. "You sure this frame is going to stick?"

Danamato lowered an eyebrow at him. "What are you talking about?"

"You turn me over to the law," Grofield said, "I might manage to put a little doubt in somebody's mind. You turn me over dead, shot trying to escape, *that'll* put doubt in somebody's mind."

Danamato shook his head in irritated confusion. "Turn you over to the law? You crazy?"

It was Grofield's turn to lower an eyebrow. "This isn't a set-up?"

They studied each other with equal incomprehension for a minute, and then Danamato slapped the table and said, "Oh, is *that* it! You been *framed!*"

"That's what it looks like," said Grofield, though he wasn't entirely sure of it any more.

"Depends where you're looking from," Danamato said. "Who's supposed to've worked this frame?"

"You," Grofield told him.

Danamato was *a*) surprised and *b*) angry. "What? How you gonna con me into that? Don't you think I *know* if—what are you trying to pull?"

"Harry is your boy."

"Sure he is."

"He waited till a patsy showed up," Grofield said. "Me."

"For what?"

"To follow out your orders," Grofield said. "To kill your wife and pin it on me. So there wouldn't be any embarrassing questions."

Danamato looked at him blank-faced for a long minute, then shook his head slowly and with an air of controlled rage threw his cigar away. Without the cigar it was a finger he had to point at Grofield. "I wanted to see you first," he said. "I wanted to ask you why you done it. I wanted to try and figure you out. But you surprise me."

"I'm glad," Grofield said.

"You come out here," Danamato said, "pushin' for an insanity plea. You out of your mind?"

"No," said Grofield.

"Then why you trying to make me angry?"

"I didn't know I was."

"I *loved* my wife!" Danamato spread his hands wide, glared up at the sky. "Belle!" he shouted. The echoes died, he kept his hands spread out, he looked at Grofield and calmly he said, "Every married couple has their misunderstandings."

Grofield wasn't sure what was what. Would Danamato really try to convince him of his innocence if he was guilty? What would be the point? He said, "Your wife thought you wanted to kill her. Was that a misunderstanding?"

"Belle exaggerated," he said. "She'd always exaggerate, Belle, she'd make a federal case out of everything."

"She was going to hire me as bodyguard," Grofield said.

"Public bodyguard, because Harry isn't pretty enough." The stir behind Grofield had to be Harry shifting his feet and glaring at the back of Grofield's neck. The other two were back there, too.

"I know about that," Danamato said. "You on horse or something?"

"Nothing," Grofield said.

"Arms."

Grofield held out his arms. The T-shirt left the arms almost completely bare, and Danamato would be able to see there were no needle marks there.

Danamato frowned. "You acted like a junkie," he said. "You pull a gun at the dinner table, Belle has to ask you please don't shoot her."

"I pulled Harry's gun on her," Grofield pointed out. "Harry had it in my back at the time. I'd been mistreated, and I was upset."

"You were upset."

"Your wife was very arrogant with me," Grofield said.

"My wife is dead," Danamato pointed out.

"That's right," Grofield said. "And you know you didn't kill her, and I know I didn't kill her."

"The hell you didn't."

Grofield said, "Think about it. It doesn't make any sense. I never saw the woman before yesterday afternoon. I was going to be leaving this morning and never see her again. Why should I kill her?"

"That's why I think you're a hophead," Danamato said. "Let me see your legs."

"My legs are clean," Grofield said. "And if there's any marks on my behind, they're from penicillin. Start talking sense, B.G."

"Who told you you could call me by name?"

"I'm not calling you by name, I'm calling you by initial. You've had my bag searched by now, haven't you? Anything in it? A needle, a packet, anything?"

"Maybe you're on LSD."

"Maybe you are," Grofield told him. "You're confused between reality and illusion."

Danamato sat back in his chair, frowning hard. The fingertips of his left hand drummed on the tabletop. From the way his cheeks were moving, he was biting them on the inside. He watched his fingertips tapping, he bit his cheeks, and he apparently did some hard thinking.

Grofield waited, watching him and doing some hard thinking of his own. Danamato hadn't ordered the killing of his wife—that seemed sure. Had Harry done it anyway, thinking it would please the boss, and was he now clamming up about it, seeing how the boss was taking it? Or was it one of the others here, after all, one of the quintet he'd already rejected earlier? Or one of the servants, teed off for some reason?

Danamato's thoughts had been taking the same route, it seemed, because finally he said, "If you didn't do it, who did?"

"You mean if I didn't and *you* didn't."

Danamato flushed with anger. Leaning forward, his tapping hand turning into a fist, he said, "I loved my wife! Dammit, I told you that already. Why do you think I sent Harry down?"

"Why does Harry think you sent him down?" Grofield asked.

Danamato didn't get it. He squinted at Grofield and said, "Hah?"

Grofield said, "Harry was around your wife all the time. She kept telling him how happy you'd be to see her dead. All the financial problems straightened out and all. So maybe after a while Harry began to think maybe she was right, maybe you'd appreciate it if he *did*—"

Grofield ducked, and Harry's swing missed his head, the barrel of the Colt gouging his flesh high on the left shoulder. He rolled off the chair, turning, kicking upward, kicking the chair into Harry, who was trying to come after him for another swing. Danamato was shouting *Harry Harry* but Harry wasn't listening, he was after Grofield.

Grofield rolled again across the slates, came up on his knees beside another of the frail-looking wrought-iron ice-cream chairs, and flung it at Harry. That gave him time to get on his feet, come inside Harry's next sweeping swing with the gun, and chop the side of his hand upward against the bottom of Harry's nose.

Harry said, "Ehhh!" He took a step back, his eyes starting to water and his nose starting to bleed, and he dropped the automatic onto the slates.

Grofield started to bend for it, but Danamato's voice cut through to him: "Stop!"

He stopped, half bent, reaching down. The other two had guns pointed at him. Danamato was on his feet, one arm extended all the way out, and he hadn't been shouting *stop* at Grofield; he'd been shouting *stop* at the other two.

Harry, both hands to his face, backed up another step, stumbled, and sat down hard on the slate. He was making a funny high-pitched noise.

Grofield straightened. He showed the other two his empty palms. They relaxed slightly, but they kept their guns in their hands.

Danamato, still standing, leaned both hands on the table, looked at Grofield and shook his head. "Not Harry," he said. "Harry was almost as fond of my wife as me. That's why I told him go with her. I told him tell her he's not working for me any more he wants to work for her. Because Harry *knows* me, and he *knows* Belle, and he *knows* I couldn't want that woman dead no matter *what!*"

"Not even Roy Chelm?" Grofield asked.

Danamato jutted out his jaw. "You're pushing, you," he said. "You keep pushing."

"What have I got to lose, B.G.?"

Danamato seemed to think about that for a second, then he nodded jerkily and said, "All right. Even Roy Chelm. You think he was the first one? Or the last?"

"The last, yes," Grofield said.

Danamato winced. "Except for what happened," he said.

"That's what I mean," said Grofield. "Maybe Roy Chelm was one too many."

"For me?"

"Maybe you. Maybe Harry. Maybe Harry thought it was one too many for you. Maybe you said something that—"

"Forget Harry!"

Grofield looked down at Harry, who had stretched out full length on his side, his legs under the table. He wasn't unconscious, but he wasn't moving. His hands were still to his face, and though the high-pitched whine had stopped, his breathing sounded like twenty asthma attacks rolled into one.

Grofield said, "If you're one hundred per cent sure it wasn't Harry, you better have somebody help him. Clean him up, put him to bed, make sure he doesn't drown on his blood."

Danamato looked down at Harry and seemed surprised, as though he hadn't realized there was anybody there. He went halfway round the table to look more closely at him, then stared at Grofield and said, "What'd you do to him?"

"I stopped him from pistol-whipping me."

"Yeah, but how?"

"I hit him," Grofield said.

Danamato looked down at Harry again and shook his head. To one of the others—the one from the Mercedes—he said, "Frank, go get a couple guys to take Harry upstairs."

Frank looked at Grofield, as though to suggest the guard on him shouldn't be cut any more, but he didn't say anything. Instead, he turned on his heel and went off into the pocket jungle. The one remaining guard began to look very alert again, his pistol trained on Grofield's mid-section.

Danamato stood over Harry studying Grofield, frowning at what he saw. "I don't know about you," he said. "I figured you were it for sure, but now I don't know."

"I'm not it," Grofield said.

"You're capable of it," Danamato said thoughtfully. "I wouldn't put anything at all past you. But you don't seem crazy, and the only reason I can think of for you to kill Belle is being crazy."

"I'm not crazy," Grofield said.

"I don't think you are." Danamato looked down at Harry again, though not as though really seeing him there. "Did somebody hire you?" he asked himself.

"No," said Grofield.

Danamato looked at him. "How come you're here?"

"Your wife sent for me. You know about that; she wanted a public bodyguard."

"My *wife* sent for you? Where'd she know you from?"

"She didn't know me."

"Then how'd she know to send for you?"

Grofield shook his head. "That wasn't how it worked," he said. "There's a South American head of state I know, a General Pozos, he—"

"Never heard of him."

"I'm not surprised. He runs a little country down there. Guerrero."

"I never heard of that either. South America?"

"South America, Central America, somewhere in there. Anyway, I know him. I was in Mexico and I got a message from him. Airline tickets here, and I should come help out a friend of his, and there'd be money in it for me."

"You're for hire?"

"Not usually." Grofield shrugged. "I was curious. The note didn't say what it was about or anything. I've scored recently. I've got enough money to carry me for a year or two. I came here mostly to find out what it was all about."

Danamato said, "You scored? What kind of score?"

"Money," Grofield said. "I take money for a living."

"What are you, a burglar?"

Grofield shook his head. "I'm in the heavy."

Danamato studied him. "You don't look it."

"Thank you."

"What've you been in on that I'd know about?"

"You know about the island casino off Texas?"

Danamato said, "You mean the night club on the island? It got burned up."

"It was a casino," Grofield said. "I helped burn it. That's the money I'm living on now."

"Then it doesn't make any sense," Danamato said. "Why come here? This isn't your line of work."

"I know. I told you, I was curious."

Danamato nibbled the insides of his cheeks again, then shook his head and said, "I don't know. I don't know about you."

"I didn't kill your wife," Grofield told him.

"And I didn't," Danamato said. "And Harry didn't. So who did?"

"I don't know."

"I want to know," Danamato said. He pointed a finger at Grofield again. "You know what I'd like to do? I'd like to just let it be you, and we bury you out in the jungle someplace, and that's the end of it."

"Not if you got the wrong man," Grofield said.

"I know." Danamato shook his head. "That's why I wanted to see you before you were taken care of. That's why I listened to you this long. That's why I let you get away with doing whatever you did to Harry."

"I hit him," Grofield said.

"I know you hit him!"

Frank came back, then, two others in his wake. They were the two Puerto Ricans who'd met Grofield yesterday. Without their shotgun and dog they seemed smaller somehow, smaller and more stupid. They picked up Harry, who gurgled when they moved him, and carried him away.

Frank unsheathed his gun again and pointed it in the general direction of Grofield.

Grofield said, "B.G., I'm getting sick of having guns pointed at me."

"That's too bad," Danamato said. "How come my wife knew this General Whatsisname?"

"Pozos."

"I don't give a damn. How come she knew him?"

Grofield shrugged. "I don't know. Maybe somebody else knew him and asked the favor for her. Milford, maybe. Or the colored guy Marba."

"I'll have to find out about that." Danamato reached into his inside pocket and took out a fresh cigar. "All right," he said. "We'll look around. If we come up with somebody else, you can go home."

"What if you don't come up with somebody else?"

Danamato paused in unwrapping the cigar. He looked at Grofield. "Don't ask foolish questions," he said.

9

His suitcase was on the bed.

"Oh, good," said Grofield, walking into the bedroom he'd used part of last night. He turned to Frank and the other one, his two-gunned escort, saying, "Do I have time to take a quick shower?"

"That's funny," said Frank. "Get dressed."

"Brush my teeth?"

"You wanna go back down right now?"

"All right," Grofield said. He opened the suitcase, saw from the disorder within that it had been searched but that nothing seemed to have been taken, and got out fresh clothing.

He changed quickly, while Frank and the other one stood impatiently in the doorway. It felt good to have shoes and a shirt on again, gave him more of a feeling of confidence, made him feel more like somebody who could handle a difficult situation.

Like this one, for instance.

"You ready?"

"Just have to powder my nose."

"Move," said Frank.

Grofield moved. He went back downstairs, the other two flanking him, and allowed them to lead him to a dining room—a smaller one than the one he'd been in last night—which Danamato had taken over as a sort of office for himself.

Danamato was at the square, heavy Mexican-style table. He motioned Grofield to sit at his right hand. Behind him were two more of his aides, one of these the bearded man who'd kidnapped Grofield yesterday, the other the one who'd used the tape recorder. Neither of them had guns showing at the moment, and the tape recorder was out in plain sight on the table, the microphone standing at an angle in a squat beige holder.

Danamato said to Grofield, "This is the way it runs. It couldn't've been any of the servants—they're out."

"Why?"

"There was two of them on guard at the foot of the stairs all night," Danamato said. "That was Milford's bright idea, on account of how easy you'd gotten in. So Belle had to be bumped by somebody already on the second floor."

Grofield nodded. "Good. I like anything that narrows it down."

"Unless it narrows it down to you," Danamato said. "You've put a doubt in my mind, buddy, but your name isn't off any list yet. In fact, it's still number one."

"I'm sorry to hear that," Grofield said.

"There was five other people up there last night," Danamato said. He had a notebook open in front of him, and he read off the list: "Roy Chelm and his sister. The Milfords. And that spade, Onum Marba. What kind of name is that?"

"African, I assume."

"Yeah." Danamato looked up from the list, studied Grofield. "Which one of the five you want ahead of you on the list?"

"That's a problem," Grofield admitted. "Frankly, Harry's still the only one I like for it."

Danamato shook his head. "It wasn't Harry. He knew the situation better than that."

"What about Milford? Didn't he know the situation? How

come he's putting guards out if he knows this is just a lover's quarrel?"

"He only knows what Belle tells him," Danamato said. "You think he's our regular lawyer? Before this divorce crap came along Milford didn't know us from nobody. He's an ambulance chaser. Belle got him on a recommendation from some divorcee friend of hers."

"It seemed to me," Grofield said, "he wasn't surprised when Harry told him he was still working for you."

"When Harry told him *who* was still working for me?"

"When Harry told him Harry was still working for you."

"Oh. He wasn't surprised?"

"It was like he'd suspected it," Grofield said. "So I still want to know, how come he put guards out when he suspected the Trojan horse was already in the gates?"

"The what?"

Grofield shook his head. "Forget it," he said. "When the time comes, I'll ask Milford." He gestured at the tape recorder. "That's the idea here, isn't it? You're going to play cop, right?"

"I'm asking these five people some questions," Danamato said. "I'm finding out if any of them ought to go ahead of you on the list."

"So you're playing cop," Grofield said. "Which is what in the theater we call daring casting. Like Mickey Rooney playing that Chinaman in *Breakfast at Tiffany's*."

Danamato frowned in confusion. "What? Mickey Rooney?"

"It doesn't matter," Grofield said. "What am I supposed to do here, just sit and observe, or can I ask questions, too?"

"You got a lot at stake here," Danamato reminded him. "You think of any questions, you go ahead and ask them."

"I've got one now," Grofield said.

"For who?"

"You."

"I thought we covered that," Danamato said.

"Different kind of question. The police haven't been called yet, have they?"

Danamato shook his head. "Not till I get this thing squared away."

"In the meantime, where's your wife?"

"There's a freezer in the basement."

Grofield looked at him. "Your wife is in there?"

Danamato met Grofield's look with a heavy look of his own. "No," he said. "That ain't Belle. Belle don't exist any more. That's a piece of meat we got to keep fresh for a while. Belle's gone." He looked away suddenly and passed his hand across his forehead and eyes. "Belle's gone," he said. "There's no place on earth that she is. And that chunk of meat ain't her, take it from me. She's no more inside that than I'm inside the suit I give to the Good Will last summer." He looked at Grofield again. "You follow me?"

"All right," Grofield said. It was odd, but until now it hadn't seemed to him real that Danamato really emotionally cared for his wife, but now that he'd heard her body was stuffed like a leg of mutton in a freezer—and he'd heard why it was possible for Danamato to treat the body like that—it was real to him. Danamato, weight and toughness and cigar and hood army and all, had honest to God loved his wife Belle. Still did. Was planning to be very hard on whoever had taken Belle away forever and left a chunk of meat in her place. Was keeping himself going simply so he could be hard on that person, whoever it was.

Grofield understood he'd damn well better help Danamato find somebody else to put on top of that list.

There was silence for half a minute or so, and then Danamato said, "You got any more questions before we get started?"

"Not just now, no," Grofield said.

"All right." Danamato looked at his list. "Let's put the spade in the front of the bus," he said. "Frank, go get him."

10

ONUM MARBA sat across the table from Danamato, his poker face as impassive as ever. He had changed to Western clothing this morning—gray slacks, gray casual shoes and a short-sleeved white shirt. What last evening's flowing robes had hidden was a strong and attractively muscled body. The arms, below the shirt sleeves, looked as hard as wood, sculptured from dark wood, almost black, with just a faint powdering of gray to keep it from shining.

In that soft, effortless voice with the faint hint of metallic clicking somewhere inside it, Marba broke the silence by saying, "It seems I am a prisoner in this house today, and that you are the one who has given the order."

"You aren't a prisoner," Danamato told him. "You just ain't leaving till we get this all straightened out. I ain't leaving, Grofield ain't leaving, you ain't leaving."

That vague impression of a smile hovered in the vicinity of Marba's lips again. Expressionlessly he said, "But I am not technically a prisoner. I see. Could you tell me why it is you sometimes say *ain't* and sometimes say *aren't?* I had not thought that individuals alternated between formal and informal speech quite so erratically in English."

Danamato stared at him in disbelief. "What the hell?"

Grofield said, "It's radio and television, Mr. Marba. The average American is influenced and affected by things all across the cultural scale. It makes for a homogeneity that can look erratic to a foreign observer."

"Thank you," said Marba, bobbing his head slightly in Grofield's direction.

Danamato was glaring at them both. "You two done?"

"I'd like to ask a question," Grofield said. "One that has to do with what we're here for."

"Then go ahead," said Danamato.

Grofield said, "Mr. Marba, are you the one who asked General Pozos to recommend someone for Belle Danamato?"

Now Marba did smile, pleasantly and reminiscently. "Yes, I did. I was happy to be of help to my hostess, if it was possible."

"You're from Africa, aren't you?"

"From Undurwa, yes."

"I never heard of that one either," said Danamato.

"I would imagine," Marba said gently, "you haven't heard of half the nations in the world. Most people haven't. Would it surprise you to hear that sixty-six of the member countries of the United Nations have populations smaller than that of New York City?"

Danamato pointed a finger at him. "Marba," he said, "you open your mouth and we're talking about something else. We're not here to talk about something else, we're here to talk about the killing of my wife."

"For which," Marba said, "I offer my condolences."

Grofield, seeing Danamato was on the verge of losing his temper, said, "I think, B.G., it's just that Marba is a politician. Politicians these days tend to talk in statistics. They got the idea from watching American politicians give press conferences." He turned to Marba. "You are in politics at home, are you not, Mr. Marba?"

Marba's smile flashed again, a cheerful and healthy thing. "I am in politics everywhere, Mr. Grofield," he said.

Grofield said, "Where do you know General Pozos from?"

"The United Nations, primarily. We met in New York, but I have been to his country. I have accompanied him also on his yacht."

"Would you say you two had much in common?"

Danamato said, "What is this?"

"It has meaning," Grofield promised him.

Marba retained some small portion of his smile, now showing pleased reflection. "Politically," he said, "I would say the General and I have much in common. We both are at the service of emerging nations, struggling for their place in the sun."

"What about personally?" Grofield asked him.

Marba's smile turned slightly sad. "General Pozos," he said, "tends to give himself over to the appetites of the flesh."

Grofield smiled back, having just heard one of the finest understatements ever spoken away from the British Isles. General Pozos was a gross man with gross appetites, a lecher, a glutton and a pig.

"As for me," Marba went on, "I'm afraid my wants are much simpler. In comparison with the good General I would say I must appear quite the ascetic."

"But you got along together."

"Politically," Marba pointed out.

"Well enough," Grofield said, "for you to think of him when Belle Danamato wanted a public escort."

Marba shrugged. "He was the only politician of note I really knew in this part of the world. Besides, it seemed to me he would be very likely to have contacts in levels of society that might produce the kind of man we were looking for." He smiled, gestured at Grofield, and said, "And, as you see, I was right."

"So you were," said Grofield sourly, thinking how much he would have preferred it if Marba had thought of somebody other than General Pozos. This mess would be somebody else's problem now.

Danamato said, "That's enough of that. I want to find out about last night."

"I'm done," Grofield said.

"Maybe you are at that," Danamato told him. To Marba he said, "What do you know about what happened last night?"

Marba shrugged slightly. "Nothing," he said.

"Nothing? You got to know something. You know my wife's dead, don't you?"

"Of course. I thought you meant information on the murderer. Did I see anyone skulking about the hall with wire in his hands, that sort of thing. I did not."

Grofield said, "Were you asleep when it happened?"

"Yes, of course. It was four in the morning."

"Was it? I didn't know how late it was. What woke you?"

"Patricia's scream."

"What did you do?"

Marba's slight smile made a brief appearance. "I sleep in the nude," he said. "I paused to don some clothing, then went out to the hall, where I saw you being marched from Mrs. Danamato's room by Harry, at the point of a gun."

Danamato said, "Were you at the dinner table when this guy threatened my wife with a gun?"

Marba met Danamato's eye. "Yes, I was. He had taken it away from Harry. I believe that was the same one Harry had after Mrs. Danamato was killed."

Danamato said, "Did it seem serious to you?"

"Did what seem serious?"

Danamato shouted, "When he threatened her with the gun!"

"At dinner? Of course not."

Danamato seemed as startled as Grofield at the answer. It was Danamato who said, "What do you mean, of course not? He had a gun on her, didn't he?"

"But he did not fire it," said Marba. "If he had fired it, that would have been serious."

Danamato took a few seconds to absorb that, and then he said, "All right. Did it seem like he *might* fire it? He ordered my wife to ask him not to shoot, didn't he?"

"I believe that was it, yes."

"Did it seem like he might shoot if she didn't do what he said?"

Marba seemed to consider for a minute, his poker face showing nothing, and then he said, "That's hard to say. Personally, I would say he intended something dramatic but harmless. A bullet through the window, perhaps, or to shoot someone's wineglass to pieces."

Grofield looked at him in some surprise. Marba had pegged it exactly; if Belle Danamato had given him a bad time at that moment, he'd have started shooting up the table, being very careful not to hit any of the people sitting at it.

"All right," Danamato was saying. "That's what you *think*. You can't be sure what he would do or wouldn't do."

"That assurance is impossible with anyone," Marba said quietly. "We are all, in the last analysis, unpredictable."

"Yeah, I'm sure we are."

Grofield said, "How long have you all been living here?"

"I have been for eleven days. Mrs. Danamato and the others for closer to a month, I believe."

Danamato looked at Grofield. "Four weeks tomorrow," he said. "Why?"

"I just wanted to know how long these people had been cooped up together," Grofield said. To Marba he said, "Mrs. Danamato hadn't left here at all, had she?"

"Not to my knowledge. Certainly not in the last eleven days."

"What about the others? Any of them go away at all?"

"Mr. Milford occasionally drives to San Juan to take care of financial or legal matters," Marba said. "Other than that, no one else has left here at all. At any rate, not in the last eleven days."

"It's a big place," said Grofield, "but not after you've been a semi-prisoner in it for a month. How have these people been getting along?"

Marba shrugged his small shrug again. "Generally well," he said. "There are always minor arguments, displays of temper and so on, when people are for a long time in one another's company, as you suggest."

"Who in particular?"

"I beg your pardon?"

Grofield rephrased it: "Which one of them has shown the most displays of temper?"

The sad smile put in another appearance. "I do dislike speaking ill of my fellow guests."

"The situation isn't normal," Grofield reminded him.

"This ain't the time to be polite," Danamato said heavily.

Marba smiled, bowed his head at Danamato, and said, "You have admirable brevity, Mr. Danamato." To Grofield he said, "I would say Roy Chelm has been the least well tempered of us all. He tends toward the . . . " He hunted for the word.

Grofield said, "Petulant?"

Marba smiled in delight. "Petulant! Precisely the word!"

"With anyone in particular?"

"With everyone. Even Mrs. Danamato on occasion, though most rarely with her. She was, after all, his protector."

"Who got along worst with Mrs. Danamato?" Grofield asked.

"I would have to say Patricia Chelm. She did not approve of the combination of her brother and Mrs. Danamato."

"Strong enough to do something about it?" Grofield asked.

"Not at all!" Marba seemed honestly shocked. "That girl? Not in the slightest."

"All right," said Grofield.

Danamato broke in to say, "What are you doing here anyway, Marba? Where's my wife know you from?"

"I introduced myself to her," Marba said. "I had heard she was interested in some particular types of investment, and I thought she might find my country congenial. We are actively seeking foreign investment, you know."

"Investment?" Danamato shook his head in bewilderment. "What kind of investment?"

"On June first," Marba said, "our country will legalize gambling. Tourism, from Europe and the British Isles and perhaps even eventually from the United States, is the economic hope of the central region of Africa, at least for the foreseeable future. It is our intention in Undurwa—"

"Wait awhile," Danamato said. "You wanted my wife to invest in a casino? In this country of yours?"

"Exactly. She seemed quite interested."

Danamato shook his head. "Christ," he said. "Of all the lame-brain—"

"I assure you," Marba said, "an investment in a casino in Undurwa will produce excellent return in the years to come. Our beaches—"

"Never mind the sales talk," Danamato said. "I'm not interested in that crap."

"Nevertheless," Marba said, "when this current business is over, and when your period of mourning is finished, I would seriously like to present our potential to you. I think it will surprise you. Did you know that—"

"No more of that!" Danamato shouted. "That's all. We don't need you any more."

"Just a minute," Grofield said. "I have one last question."

Danamato looked at him with heavy disapproval. "Get it over with," he said.

Grofield said to Marba, "Mr. Marba, it's been established that one of us up on the second floor has to be the murderer. That means only six of us."

Marba nodded. "Yes, I know."

"Who's your candidate?" Grofield asked him. "Who do you think did it?"

"Frankly," Marba said, "I have difficulty in believing it of any of us."

"So do I. But it had to be one of us. There's no other choice. So which one is your pick?"

Marba's smile was very, very sad. "I'm afraid it would have to be you, Mr. Grofield," he said.

11

ROY CHELM came in angry and petulant, high color in both cheeks. Pointing at Frank, one of his escorts, he said, "That gorilla slapped my sister! Knocked her down!" He was outraged.

Danamato looked calmly at Frank. "What was the matter?"

Frank looked bored. "She wasn't going to let us take her little brother away. She was going to come along, or Roysy Poysy couldn't go."

"He struck her!" shouted Chelm.

Danamato gave him a long flat look, then said, "How old are you, Chelm?"

"What difference does that make? He struck my—"

"Frank," Danamato said loudly, drowning Chelm out, "take this punk out of here and beat the crap out of him. When he's ready to answer questions, bring him back in."

"Right," said Frank, and reached for Chelm's elbow.

"Wait!" cried Chelm, ducking away, backing into another of Danamato's men, who grabbed him from behind by both arms.

Danamato looked at him. "You ready to calm down?" he asked.

"I . . . " said Chelm. He swallowed, struggled for self-control, finally nodded his head convulsively. "Yes," he said.

"Good." Danamato motioned, saying, "Let him go, Jack," and Jack let him go.

Chelm staggered, losing his balance, but then caught it again. Danamato said to him, "I asked you before, how old are you?"

"Twenty—twenty-seven."

"And how old's your sister?"

"Twenty-two."

Danamato looked disgusted. "Then it's time you got out from behind her," he said. "Sit down."

Chelm, pulling his tattered remnants of dignity around himself like a wino in the park protecting himself from the winter wind with two sheets of yesterday's newspaper, sat down in the chair Onum Marba had vacated and said, "My sister and I have been inseparable since—"

"Crap," Danamato said. "You came down here with my wife?"

The word *wife* seemed to give Chelm a start. His eyes widened perceptibly and stayed wider. "We all did," he said. "All except Marba, of course."

"You were the boy friend, right?"

"We were engaged," Chelm said, his voice a bit shaky.

Danamato smiled grimly. "Engaged," he said.

"We were going to get married," Chelm said with that kind of terror that tries to hide as defiance. "As soon as she got her divorce from you."

"Which would have been never, kid," Danamato said. "You think you were the first gigolo she hit me over the head with? Three days I'd have to be in Las Vegas, that's all, not even touch one of them chorines, and in the mail I'd get a picture of her and some male model at the Copa."

"It wasn't like that at all," announced Chelm, trying for dignity.

"Yeah, yeah, kid," Danamato said, shutting him up again. "I know all about how it was, and how you thought it was, and all the rest of it." He turned to Grofield, saying, "The same as talking to that clown, Marba. She'd carry on like it was real, right down to the wire, but when push came to shove she'd never go through with it."

"Maybe," Grofield said.

"Who knew her?" Danamato demanded. "You or me?"

"Neither of you," Chelm said with shaky defiance. When Danamato turned to stare at him in amazement, Chelm told him, "All she was to you was a body to take out your tempers on. Sex if you felt like sex. Anger if you felt angry. You never knew the *real* Belle, you never knew the soft woman inside, the one that cringed every time—"

Danamato came off his chair like a bull, lunging across the table, the microphone and tape recorder flying, his outstretched hands closing on Chelm's throat. The two of them went crashing to the floor, Danamato on top, Chelm flailing ineffectually beneath him. Chelm's face was turning red.

Grofield leaned back in his chair and smiled across the room at Frank, who with the others was staring in confusion, not sure what to do. "There they are, boys," Grofield said cheerfully. "A couple of feeble-minded high-schoolers. Two teenagers fighting it out over a piece of frozen meat in the basement."

The two on the floor stopped thrashing around. Danamato's fingers loosened on Chelm's throat. Chelm lay unmoving on his back, staring up in horror, afraid to move, while Danamato got up to his knees, holding to the table edge, and glowered at Grofield. "You son of a bitch," he said hoarsely.

Grofield smiled pleasantly at him. "How old are you, B.G.?" he asked.

Danamato gripped hard to the table. Grofield watched him, knowing Danamato was doing his best not to jump Grofield next. Grofield wished him the best of luck.

Everybody won. Danamato let go pent-up breath, nodded, and got to his feet. "All right, Grofield," he said. "You're right." He glared around at his troops. "What was the matter with you guys? Why didn't you get me off this piece of shit?"

They all looked worried and helpless. Grofield said, "You surrounded yourself with yes men, B.G. Dangerous thing to do."

Danamato shook his head, adjusted his suit coat, and walked around the table to pick up his chair. "Get that turd out of here," he said. "I got nothing more to ask him."

"I have," Grofield said.

"You would," Danamato said. "All right, Frank, Jack, put him back in his chair."

They helped Chelm to his feet. His face was no longer red; it was ashen white. He allowed himself to be lifted and then put in the chair, and he sat there as though he was brittle.

Grofield said, "Chelm?"

Chelm looked at him but didn't answer.

Grofield said, "Are you receiving, Chelm? Can you hear me?"

Chelm nodded. "Yes," he said. His voice sounded rusty, and he put a hand to his throat as though the throat hurt.

"Good," Grofield said. "Tell me something. When did Belle Danamato tell you she wasn't going to marry you after all, she was going back to her husband instead? Was it before I got here yesterday, or after?"

Chelm's face went from white to grayish green. Hoarsely he said, "What are you trying to do? You know that isn't true."

"Isn't it? Only Mrs. Danamato could tell us for sure, couldn't she? You put a lot of hope into this marriage, didn't you? All that Danamato money."

"I loved Belle!" The hoarse shout cracked midway through.

"Sure you did," Grofield said. "Even after she told you it was all over, she was going back to her husband."

"She never did! She wouldn't have, not Belle! We were going to get married!" Chelm was suddenly on his feet, pointing a shivering finger at Grofield, shouting, "Don't think I can't see what you're up to! Trying to pin this on somebody else, anybody else, just to save your own skin."

"Can you think of a better reason?" Grofield asked him. He turned to Danamato, saying, "Does it make sense? You're sure she'd come back to you eventually. Roy here was banking on the marriage. So maybe she told him it was all up, the bad time I gave her at dinner shook her up and she wanted you again, the playacting was all done. What would a petulant little boy like Roy do in a situation like that? What does a petulant little boy do when he's told he can't play with a favorite toy any more? He breaks it."

Danamato watched Chelm. "This one?" he said.

"You've got contempt for him," Grofield said. "Why not? You should have contempt for him. But don't underrate him. He'd be a nasty little boy if he could get the drop on you."

Chelm leaned over the table toward Danamato, shouting, "Can't you see what he's trying to do? Can't you see what he's up to? He wants to frame somebody, anybody, to get himself off the hook. *He* was the one who threatened her, not me! And it was right after *he* got here that she was killed!"

"All right," Danamato said heavily. "We'll think about it."

"*He's* the one!"

"I told you I'll think about it! Frank, get him outa here. Bring his sister in."

Chelm's arm was taken by Frank, but he kept shouting, kept pointing the finger of his free hand at Grofield until the door shut behind him.

Danamato studied Grofield. "Do you believe it yourself?"

"I don't have to believe it," Grofield told him truthfully. "What he said just now is absolutely right. I've got to find somebody else to get me off the hook. The difference is, I'm the one being framed. The easiest way to get that somebody else who'll get me off the hook is with the truth. But I'm not particular, B.G., I'll tell you the God's own truth. If I can't figure out who really did kill your wife, I'll settle for somebody who looks good. I'd frame you if it would do me any good."

Danamato grinned crookedly. "You use truth like a weapon, don't you?" he said.

Grofield showed him empty hands. "It's the only one I've got right now," he said.

12

PATRICIA CHELM was as unreachable and self-contained as a turtle in its shell. She sat rigid in the chair opposite Danamato, knees together, hands folded in lap, head straight, shoulders back. She was wearing a pale-blue skirt, a little too long to be in style, and a plain white blouse. She had a model's figure, small-breasted, slender almost to the point of skinniness, and the face of a Vassar undergraduate smelling a dead cat.

She said, her voice cold, her eyes glaring at Danamato, "I have a statement to make."

"That's wonderful," Danamato said. "Go ahead, make it."

"If you make the mistake of leaving any of us alive," she said, "I assure you we will exert every effort to see to it that you do not get away with this. You attacked my brother, physically attacked him. He has bruises all over his throat. One of your hoodlums struck me. We have been detained against our will, though I have insisted repeatedly that someone be instructed to drive my brother and me to San Juan."

Grofield said, "Don't you drive?"

She ignored him, concentrating her attention on Danamato. "I demand," she said, "that we be permitted to leave at once. We are sorry for Mrs. Danamato's death, of course, but you have captured her murderer and you have no reason or right to detain us any longer. We have—"

Grofield said, "How old were you when your brother first showed it to you?"

Her head snapped around, her eyes stared at him, her face turned beet red. "I . . . " She shook her head, brought one hand halfway to her face and let it drop again. "I have no idea what you're talking about," she said.

"You have a red face, lady," Grofield said.

She did touch her face now and apparently found it hot, because she pulled her fingers away at once. She looked desperately back at Danamato saying shakily, "We insist that we be driven—"

"So you have a letch for your brother," said Grofield calmly. "There's nothing wrong with that—it happens all the time. Of course, you don't want it to take charge of your life."

To Danamato she said, "I shouldn't be required to sit here and listen, listen, I shouldn't have to listen to—"

"Psychologically," Grofield said, "it's easy to figure. Partly it's maternal, getting the wife and mother roles confused in the family relationship. You were always the little mother, even though he was five years older. And partly it's self-protection, keeping yourself safely out of adult relationships by continuing to be hung up on your brother. Then there's—"

"I'm not going to . . . " She was on her feet, cheeks and eyes blazing.

"Sit down, lady," said Danamato. "Sit down or I'll have Frank sit you down."

She jerked her head around at Frank, then quickly sat down.

"As I was saying," Grofield said, "there's also the virgin's fear of the male. And if there's a twenty-two-year-old virgin anywhere in the Caribbean, honey, it's you."

"Please," she said, still to Danamato. She extended one hand part way across the table. Her expression was tragic now, her voice broken. "Please don't let him do that. Why should he do that? What good does it do anybody to have him talk like that?"

Danamato turned to Grofield. "Well? What's it all about?"

Grofield said, "Look at her. Compare her with your wife. Your wife was all blood and guts; she was alive when she was alive. She might have irritated me, she might have been over-bearing, but she was vital. And look at this one. You couldn't find enough blood in her veins to make a scab."

Patricia Chelm shook her head spastically, opening and closing her mouth but not saying anything.

Danamato studied her broodingly. "All right," he said. "I got no argument with anything you said, but what's the point?"

"The point is," said Grofield, "this one has sacrificed herself to her brother. The sacrifice was a cop-out on life, but still she'd think of it as a sacrifice. A big gift of herself to her brother. So what does he do? He goes out and gets himself engaged to Marjorie Main."

"Marjorie Main? Belle didn't look—"

"I know. I'm doing comparisons. Meat and potatoes on one side, thin beer on the other. How do you think this one felt when she first met her brother's bride-to-be? Fifteen years older than him. Loud. Boisterous. Crude. Common. A divorcee. In fact, not even a divorcee—not yet."

"Hmmmm," said Danamato.

"I liked Belle very much," Patricia Chelm said, but the statement lacked a certain zing.

"Sure you did," said Grofield.

"Only a fool," she said, "would think me capable of doing such a thing as—I can't even speak of it."

"I can," said Grofield. "You'd stood it as long as you could, hating Belle Danamato more every day. Yesterday at dinner, when I pointed the gun at her, I saw the expression on your face, and you *wanted* me to shoot."

"That's a lie!"

Grofield didn't know if it was a lie or not, he didn't care. He had his own skin to worry about; let everybody else worry about their own on their own time. At the very least he could sow confusion, which might be helpful, and at the very best he could convince Danamato that *somebody* else had killed his wife.

Which was the only truth he was interested in. Somebody else, one of these five people, had killed Belle Danamato. Which one did it was up to somebody besides Alan Grofield. What Grofield had to do was find one of them that Danamato would accept as the killer.

So he went on now, saying, "You were sorry when I didn't shoot Belle Danamato at dinner, and it was after that you decided to do the job yourself. You figured I'd get the blame for it, so the timing couldn't be better. You'd have your sweet brother all to yourself again, and think how much you could console him for the loss of his fiancée."

"That's vicious!" she cried. "That's vicious and evil and untrue, and you know it!"

Grofield waved a lazy hand. "Your witness," he said.

She appealed to Danamato again, saying, "You can't believe—"

"What were you doing in my wife's room at four in the morning?" Danamato asked her.

"Good question!" said Grofield happily.

"I couldn't sleep," she said. "I'd been asleep, but I had nightmares, so I got up and I couldn't get back to sleep. I was troubled about this man here. I didn't think he should be trusted under our roof at all. In fact, it was him I had the nightmares about."

"I don't think I like you dreaming about me," Grofield said.

"Shut up," Danamato told him. "So you couldn't sleep," he said to Patricia Chelm. "So what?"

"I went to talk to Belle. She was frequently awake late herself. She was an insomniac."

Danamato nodded heavily. "That's right. Pills, always pills."

"She was trying not to take them any more," she said. "She said it was only because you'd made her so nervous over the years that she'd had to take pills in the first place, and then they'd gotten to be a habit, and now she was trying to break the habit."

Danamato obviously didn't like that, but he didn't say anything about it. Instead, he said, "So you went in to see her, is that it?"

"I saw the light on. The door was slightly open, the way she usually left it. I pushed it open the rest of the way, and saw her there, and . . . " She began to blink very rapidly.

"All right," Danamato said gruffly. "We know about it after that. That's all the questions." He looked at Grofield. "You?"

"Not me," said Grofield.

"Take her back, Frank," Danamato said. "And bring me that shyster lawyer."

"Before I go," she said.

They all looked at her.

She sat prim again, most of the unfortunate color once more gone from her cheeks. She was looking at Danamato. She said, "That man there made an innuendo I want to answer. He implied my brother was . . . sleeping with Belle Danamato. He was not. He certainly would not, and neither would she, not before the marriage. Only the most evil mind could—"

Danamato shouted, "What? Are you out of your head?"

Amazed, she stared at him. "Why? What?"

Danamato pointed at Frank. "Take her away," he said quickly, "but hold the lawyer a minute. I want the brother again first."

"Right," said Frank.

Patricia Chelm was still bewildered. "But . . . I . . . what?"

Frank took her by the arm and she allowed herself to be led from the room.

Grofield looked at Danamato. "Out of character, huh?"

"The brother's got to have given her a snow job," Danamato said. "I know Belle. I was the only thing permanent in her life, I know that for sure, but there was a hell of a lot of temporary this and that."

"If they weren't sleeping together," Grofield said, "maybe it *was* for real this time. And maybe Harry knew it, and he decided you—"

"Lay off Harry! You're trying to pin it on everybody!"

"I'm trying to pin it on *somebody*."

"How come you didn't try it with the spade? Couldn't think of anything?"

"That depends," Grofield said. "How important was her investment to him politically at home? If he'd staked his political future on her pumping money into the country, and if she told him last night the joy ride was over, she wasn't getting divorced, she wasn't going to have money of her own to throw around, it could just be he lost his temper and gave her better than he'd got. These repressed types that always show a cool façade, they're usually a volcano underneath; if the façade finally does get broken they explode all over the place." Grofield nodded. "Oh, it could have been him, all right," he said.

Danamato stared at him, astonished. "Jesus," he said. "You really do wing it, don't you?"

"The funny part of it is," Grofield said, "one of these ad libs is the truth. Because, B.G., *I did not kill your wife.* That part happens to be true, which means one of these other people did the job, which means one of the things I'm suggesting is also the truth."

"Which one?"

"I don't know yet."

Frank returned then, leading Roy Chelm by the arm. Chelm was just as terrified as before.

Danamato fixed him with a steely eye. "I got one question," he said.

Grofield put his hand on Danamato's forearm. When Danamato looked at him questioningly, Grofield leaned over and whispered in his ear, "Let me ask it. He hears the question from you, he'll go up the wall. We'll never get anything out of him."

"Yeah," said Danamato. "Okay, go ahead."

Grofield looked at Chelm. "The question's a delicate one," he said. "Don't be scared, nobody's going to start choking you. But we need a straight answer on this one. It's important."

"I'll naturally—" Chelm stopped and coughed and cleared his throat—"do what I can," he finished.

"Good." Grofield hesitated, phrasing it properly in his head, and then said, "As close as you can remember, on what date did you first go to bed with Belle Danamato?"

Chelm's face had already been bloodless. Now it looked flesh-less, too, as though blue-gray skin had been stretched over gray-white bones. "I . . . " he said in a shrill whisper.

Danamato, his own voice gruff, said, "I ain't going to slug you. You can tell the truth."

Chelm's head was shaking back and forth like a hypnotist's watch. "Never," he gasped. "Never. I—never. We agreed, we—we both said . . . we wouldn't think of—we wanted to do this right, do it *right!* To be honest, to do everything *properly!* Not till we were *married!*"

It was the truth. If ever truth had come spurting out of any man on the face of the earth, this was the time. Chelm's face, Chelm's voice, Chelm's twitching body, all attested to it. He and Belle Danamato, his fiancée, had never gone to bed together.

"Christ on a crutch," Danamato whispered. He shook his head, then waved at Frank. "Take it away," he said. "Put it back in the butterfly case. And bring me the lawyer."

Frank and the sputtering, still-denying Chelm left the room. Danamato and Grofield looked at each other. Grofield said, "So maybe it was different this time."

"I don't get it," Danamato said.

"I hate to keep harping on Harry—"

"Just shut up," Danamato said.

13

GEORGE MILFORD sat more or less relaxed in the chair across the table from Danamato and said, "I've had a lot of dealings with your attorneys, of course, but this is my first meeting with you. I'm truly sorry it had to be under circumstances such as these."

"Sure," said Danamato.

Milford looked at Grofield. "How are you? Holding up fairly well, I hope, all things considered."

"All things considered," said Grofield.

"You really got caught up in a whirlpool here, I'm afraid," Milford said.

Danamato said quickly, "What's the matter? Don't you think he's the one did the job?"

"Grofield?" Milford shook his head. "Of course not. The man had no reason to."

"He threatened her at the dinner table."

"Nonsense," said Milford. "I was there, you weren't. That

was grandstanding, not a threat. That isn't your murderer, Danamato."

Danamato lowered his eyebrows at him. "Yeah? Then who is?"

Milford shook his head, shrugged his shoulders, negligently spread his hands. "I have no idea. But it isn't Grofield."

"Maybe it's you."

Milford smiled a thin forgiving smile. "Afraid not," he said. "I had no motive."

Danamato looked at Grofield. "Well? You want to try fitting him?"

Grofield smiled at Milford. "Not me," he said. "If Mr. Milford thinks I'm innocent, I'm willing to return the favor. I don't think Mr. Milford killed his client because I don't think he had any reason to. In fact, the more I think about it, the more I think it was Harry."

"Shut up about Harry!"

Milford, quite earnest, said to Grofield, "Oh, no, not Harry. He was devoted to Belle. He was terribly shocked by her death."

Danamato said to Milford, "It was one of you people on the second floor. You set that up yourself, putting them two spics on guard downstairs. So if it wasn't Grofield and it wasn't you—" he looked at Grofield—"and it wasn't Harry—" he looked back at Milford—"then who was it?"

"Marba?"

Danamato lowered his head but kept studying Milford. "Why? Why him?"

Milford shrugged again, casually. "He's black."

"So what?"

"You don't like that? The hot-headed black man?"

Grofield laughed aloud. "Milford," he said, "this is serious."

Danamato looked beetle-browed at the two of them. "What's going on? You two know each other from someplace?"

"We met yesterday," Milford said. "And what about the fact that Belle wasn't going to give Marba any money?"

Danamato cocked his head. "Who says?"

"She did."

"To you or to him?"

"To me yesterday just after lunch. Whether she told him last night or not I can't say."

Grofield said, "Did she tell anybody else?"

"I don't know. Probably not."

Danamato looked at Grofield. "What do you think of it?"

Grofield shook his head. "I don't know. I'd prefer to believe Mr. Milford in everything, of course, since he gave me such a vote of confidence, but I'm not sure about this. It's a little too neat."

"I can't help that," Milford said.

Danamato said, "We could ask Marba."

Grofield said, "It wouldn't do any good."

"Why not?"

"He'll say he knew nothing about it. Which could mean any one of three different things. First, that Milford is lying. Second, that Milford is telling the truth, but Mrs. Danamato hadn't gotten around to giving Marba the word yet. Third, that Marba was told but is lying. And even if it is number three, it doesn't mean he killed her. He could just be trying to avoid trouble."

Milford said, "You left out the Mr."

Grofield smiled at him. "I know. I was speaking objectively. Do you mind if I ask you a question?"

"Not at all."

"You became Mrs. Danamato's attorney recently, didn't you?"

"Yes. A little over a month ago."

"When she left her husband."

Milford nodded.

Grofield said, "Forgive me, Mr. Milford, but it seems as though you couldn't have had much of a practice back home if you could leave it for a month like this."

Milford made a smile almost as sour as Danamato's expression. "Not much of a practice," he said. "To tell the truth, not any practice at all."

"You were retired?"

Milford sighed. "All right," he said. "I didn't really think I could avoid talking about it. There was a scandal, as a result of which my name wasn't worth much in the legal profession."

"A legal scandal?"

"Not exactly. I left my wife for a girl."

Grofield said, "A girl?"

Milford closed his eyes. "All *right*. A high-school girl. We were gone seven weeks, we . . . It wasn't anybody's fault, we . . ." He opened his eyes again, looked at Danamato. "Your wife knew about it," he said. "A friend of mine sent her to me. He was kind enough to say that although I was incredibly stupid in my personal life I was still a good lawyer. And I would be able to devote the amount of time to her problems that she required."

"Were all the problems legal?" Grofield asked.

Milford looked at him with frowning distaste. "What is that supposed to mean?"

"I was wondering," Grofield said, "if your extracurricular interests were limited to high-school girls."

Milford was on his feet. "Grofield," he said, "in your own quiet, amiable way you're a filthy bastard."

"Just wondering," Grofield said.

"And I'm wondering," Milford told him, "if I was wrong to exonerate you from Belle's death quite so hastily."

Grofield smiled. "Thank you, Mr. Milford," he said. "I didn't feel right going after you with that hanging over my head." He turned to Danamato. "You knew your wife," he said. "You knew she wasn't likely to be a celibate. There wasn't anything doing with Roy Chelm, so where was it coming from? It had to be one of three. Harry. Marba. Or the terror of the schoolyard here."

"Grofield," Milford said, his voice shaking, "you're going too far."

"I can't go too far," Grofield told him. "I have a noose around my neck."

"Let me suggest an alternative," Milford said angrily. "Belle wasn't sleeping with *anyone* here. Not Harry. Not Marba. And certainly not me. I'll remind you my wife is with me, even if I had the desire, even if Belle had the desire, in these close quarters it would have been impossible."

"Not impossible," Grofield said. "Tough, but not impossible. You could have done it, counselor. If you could cut one little nubbin out of the kind of pack high-school girls travel in, you could—"

"Shut up!" Milford shouted. He was still on his feet, and he was obviously thinking about taking a lunge at Grofield.

Danamato said, "Milford. You said something about an alternative."

Milford weaved a bit, as though his balance had been strained too much by his desire to leap. Then he took a deep breath, looked at Danamato again, and said, "Yes. I believe Belle was coming around to the realization that she could never marry Roy. I don't know that she planned to go back to you, but I think she was through with Roy, or was going to be soon. And I'll swear she wasn't carrying on with anyone else here. But she did suddenly ask for a presentable man. For public appearances, she said, but maybe for private appearances, too. Maybe what she really wanted Grofield for was bed duty, and she approached him about it last night after we'd all gone to bed. She was direct and straightforward, she might have gone to his room—"

Danamato said, "She was found in her own room."

"I'll come to that," Milford said. "You know the kind of temper Grofield can have. He showed it at dinner last night. So Belle woke him, she wanted stud service, he got his back up, they argued, he got enraged and killed her. Then he carried the body back to its own room, went back to bed, and waited for somebody else to discover her."

There was silence. In it, Danamato turned and smiled heavily at Grofield, saying, "All of a sudden we got a motive."

"Amazing," Grofield said. "A woman with Belle Danamato's appetites, she spends a month in the same house with a man with a recent sex scandal in his past, she even hired him because of it, and not once does she make a play for him. I'm amazed."

"My wife was with me," Milford said. "If she hadn't been, I don't say nothing would have happened. I came to care for Belle very much. But Eva was with me, and nothing happened."

"Maybe," Grofield said. He looked at Danamato. "It's still maybe," he said. "Maybe me, maybe Milford, maybe one of the others. You still don't have enough to be sure."

"But you're still on top of the list," Danamato said.

Grofield nodded. "Sad but true. I'm done with Humbert Humbert if you are."

"Who?"

"Milford."

Milford smiled at Grofield and shook his head. "Never try to frame a lawyer," he said.

"I'll remember that," Grofield promised him.

14

EVA MILFORD was an overwound mainspring. Her hairdo was so tight and rigid it looked as though it had been set by the Spanish Inquisition. Her torso didn't look girdled, it looked petrified, like an old forest. Her dark-brown suit and fussy coral blouse made her look like the mean old broad in the steno pool, and her face was as shut up as a bank on Sunday.

She came in and remained standing. Unbelievably, she had a pocketbook clutched in both hands, over her stomach. She looked like an indignant mother coming to get her juvenile delinquent out of the precinct house. "I want to go home," she said, and she sounded indignant, too. "I've had enough of this, and I want to go home."

"There's a dead woman in this house," Danamato started portentously.

"Down in the freezer, as a matter of fact," Grofield said pleasantly.

It startled her, as it was supposed to do. She looked at Grofield wide-eyed, but said nothing.

Danamato glowered briefly at Grofield, then looked back at Eva Milford. "The point is," he said, "she's here. And she's dead. And nobody's going home, nobody's going anywhere, till I'm sure who did it."

"Well, *I* didn't do it, and my *husband* certainly—"

"Sure you did," Grofield said.

She stared at him again. "What? What?"

"You suspected your husband was up to his shenanigans again," Grofield said. "You suspected it for a couple of weeks, didn't you?"

"My husband promised me—"

"That just made it worse," Grofield said. "When he broke that solemn promise he'd made after the high-school girl, when he went—"

"He didn't break it! What are you saying?"

"I'm saying," Grofield told her, "that after you saw your husband come out of Belle Danamato's room last night, you went in there with every intention of murdering her. First you hit her with something, knocking her out, and then you wrapped that wire around her neck."

"Me? *Me?*" One hand clutching her pocketbook, the other clutching the back of the chair she hadn't sat down in, Eva Milford tottered there, staring in horror and disbelief at Grofield.

Grofield turned casually to Danamato. "Look at her," he said. "Guilt is written all over her."

Danamato didn't look at Eva Milford; he looked at Grofield. "You never stop, do you?" he said. "This woman? Look at her, for Christ's sake!"

"You don't think she'd kill to keep her husband? Look at her face, her clothes. Look how she holds that purse. You think she's just a sweet little matronly lady? That woman's a volcano. She's one of these repressed bitches starts punching a bus driver every once in a while. You look at her, Danamato. You think I'm making this up?"

Danamato finally did turn his eyes to Eva Milford, in time to see the gradual transition from shock to anger. Her eyes were small and very pale and full of hate as she glared at Grofield. Danamato thoughtfully said, "You're making it up, all right, but that doesn't mean it isn't maybe true anyway."

"You bastard!" Eva Milford screamed and came rushing at Grofield with her pocketbook swinging.

Grofield rolled out of the chair, grabbing her by the off-wrist as he did so and turning her into the table. She fell across it, the pocketbook narrowly missing Danamato, and Grofield ducked around behind Jack, who was standing there with his mouth open.

Jack spun around and grabbed Grofield in his arms, shouting, "Where the hell you going?"

"Away from her," Grofield told him.

Meantime, Frank and one of the other guards had grabbed Eva Milford and were holding her pinned in front of the table. She was shrieking various words and trying to throw her pocketbook at Grofield.

Grofield called over her noise at Danamato, "There! Is *that* an admission of guilt?"

"Get her out of here!" Danamato bellowed, and Eva Milford was dragged away.

In the silence that followed, Jack reluctantly released Grofield, who went back over and sat down in his old chair, saying, "Did you notice something interesting? Sooner or later everybody calls me a bastard."

"That's not hard to figure," Danamato said.

Grofield reached for Danamato's notebook, saying, "Let's take a look at this list. As I see it, everybody has a motive of one sort or another. Let's see if we can figure out a most probable."

Danamato pulled his notebook back. "You," he said.

Grofield shook his head. "No. I didn't do it. What about—"

"I'll do my thinking without you," Danamato told him. To Jack he said, "Put this one upstairs in his room. Lock him in."

Grofield said, "What for?"

"I'm going to think things out," Danamato said. "When I'm

done thinking, somebody around here is going to die. So far, I think it's you. I'll let you know when I'm a hundred per cent sure. Jack, take him up."

Grofield got to his feet. "Could I ask a favor?"

"What?"

"I still haven't had anything to eat. I've done all this on an empty stomach, and believe me by now I'm pretty hungry."

Danamato smiled unpleasantly. "You want a hearty meal? Sure. Jack, take him to the kitchen first, get him something to eat, then upstairs."

"Thanks," said Grofield.

"*Bon appetit*," said Danamato.

15

THE windows were ornately barred, in the Spanish manner. The purpose was primarily decorative, but they were strong iron bars, strongly implanted in the outer wall of the house, combining decoration with function in a way pleasing to the aesthetic sense and disgusting to Grofield in the extreme.

Down there were two cars, the black Mercedes he'd first seen yesterday and a turquoise-and-white Pontiac. Though one or another of Danamato's men occasionally passed by that area, the outside of the house didn't seem to be under consistent guard. If he could get out of this room and downstairs and into one of those cars, it wouldn't take long to jump the wires and get the hell out of here.

Escape seemed the best bet for survival, all things considered. Grofield knew damn well it was one of the other six people up here last night who'd done that murder, but he also knew that they all had potential motives and possible opportunities, and no one loomed any larger—particularly in Danamato's mind—than any other. Except himself, of course.

Was anything going to change that? Was Danamato going to play back his tape recording of the questions and answers and come up with any new answer of his own? Grofield went over what he could remember of the session, and there didn't seem to be anything there. Nothing that said this one or that one. Nothing that said anyone except Grofield, not for Danamato.

Out. If he was going to go on living, it had to be somewhere other than here. But how?

He was wrapped up nicely in this box, waiting for Danamato to decide it was time to unwrap him. There were the two windows, both barred and impossible. There were two doors, one to the closet and one to the hall. The closet was just a closet, and the hall door was locked. He'd fiddled with the knob; he'd tried slipping a piece of cardboard between door and frame to pop the lock, and it just wasn't going to happen. The hinges were inside where they couldn't be gotten at, and the door was heavy solid wood.

There had been three of them come for him the last time, and he could see no reason they'd cut the odds next time. Three of them, all pros, all armed, all wary. And what did he have against them?

He could throw his suitcase at them.

Wonderful.

Grofield prowled the room, trying to think and having too many things to think about all at once. He'd start thinking about ways out of this room, and in the middle he'd find himself thinking instead about Marba or Roy Chelm or Eva Milford and did one of *them* do it? So he'd concentrate on that, and pretty soon he'd be at the open window, inspecting the bolts holding the bars in place.

The problem was, he had two problems to think about and both of them seemed insoluble. He could neither find a way out of here nor a definite indication of who had killed Belle Danamato. Failing on both fronts, he was bobbing back and forth between the two like a tennis ball on a September afternoon.

This wasn't where he belonged. He wasn't a loner; he worked with a string. If he was acting, there was the rest of the cast working with him, and if he was on a robbery it was always with a group, working to a prearranged plan. This was an unusual experience for him, working as a solo and having to ad-lib his part, and so far he didn't think much of his performance. He'd managed to accomplish nothing but make things steadily worse for himself, like a man tap dancing in quicksand.

There was a click at the door. A key in the lock.

Grofield had been at the window again, gloomily studying the solidly encased bolts and thinking about his deficiencies at improvisational living. When he heard the key in the lock, he moved quickly away from the window, around the bed, and stopped beside the door, where he would be behind it when it opened. He might as well go down kicking.

The door opened slowly, stopping when it was barely open a foot. Then nothing happened for several years, while Grofield stood on the balls of his feet, his hands opening and closing at his sides.

Then a whisper whispered, "Mr. Grofield?"

Female.

Grofield reached around the door at approximate head height, found hair, closed his fingers in it, and yanked, simultaneously slamming the door with his shoulder.

The door just missed her as she came tottering in, crying *ouch!* and following Grofield's tugging hand. Grofield let her go, she half spun around and tripped over the bed, and Grofield stood with his back to the door, looking at her.

Patricia Chelm. She was sprawled over the bed, off which she got as soon as she got her balance back. Face flushed a healthy color, she struggled to her feet, frantically smoothed her skirt, and backed away from him, whispering harshly, "What's the matter with you? Why did you do that?"

"I'm nervous," Grofield told her. The key she'd dropped was on the floor near him. He picked it up and pocketed it. "The visit pleases me, naturally," he said. "What prompts it?"

"We want you to help us," she said. She was under somewhat better control by now.

"We?"

"Roy and I."

"How do I help you two?"

"You drive us away from here."

"Why me?"

"You were right before," she said. "Downstairs. We can't drive, neither of us."

"Everybody can drive," he said.

She shook her head. "My father doesn't believe in some things. Like television. Automobiles."

"How do you get around?"

"Taxi. Or walk."

Grofield shook his head. "All right," he said. "It takes all kinds. So you need a chauffeur."

"Yes," she said. "And you need to get away from here. Mr. Danamato hasn't been fooled, you know. He still knows you killed his wife."

"I didn't."

"Of course you did," she said. "But I don't care. We have to get away from here, and so do you, so we'll join forces for a while."

Grofield studied her guardedly. "Why do you have to get away from here?"

"Roy does. Because of Mr. Danamato."

"Why?"

"You don't think Mr. Danamato would let Roy leave here alive, do you?"

"Yes," said Grofield.

"Well, you're wrong," she said. "Roy took his wife away from him. Besides, we'll know about his killing you, we'll be dangerous witnesses, we'll know too much."

Grofield was sure Danamato had worked that part out, and he knew Danamato wasn't hot for revenge against the celibate lover, but on the other hand it was Patricia Chelm's mistaken beliefs along these lines that had brought her here to offer Grofield his life back on a silver platter, so it didn't make too much sense to argue her into a true understanding of the situation. Therefore, Grofield said, "I see what you mean. So you want me to help you two get away."

"We'll help each other," she said. "I get you out of this room, you drive the car."

"It's a deal," he said. "Which car?"

"I have the keys to Mr. Milford's car."

"The Pontiac?"

"The turquoise-and-white one, yes."

"It's a Pontiac," Grofield said.

"It is? Well, anyway, we ought to get started, shouldn't we?"

"Where's Roy?"

"Hiding in the car," she said. Then she smiled coldly and said, "No, Mr. Grofield, you aren't going to overpower me and take the keys and make your getaway alone."

Grofield had had plans along those lines. He grinned and shrugged and said, "Oh, well. You win a few, you lose a few. Just let me close my suitcase, and I'm with you."

"You're going to take your suitcase?"

"My Gleem is in there. You want me to get cavities?"

Grofield shut the suitcase, hefted it and went over to the door. He opened it and peeked out and the hall was empty. He motioned to Patricia Chelm, and she followed him out to the hall.

The stairs were down at the end of the hall, where it turned to the right. They met no one in the hall and no one on the stairs, but as they reached the foot of the stairs they heard voices approaching.

"In here!" Grofield said, heading for the nearest shut door.

It was a closet, containing brooms and raincoats. They squeezed in together, the suitcase helping fill the space to overflowing, and shut the door behind themselves.

In the dark, it was hard to remember what a neuter Patricia Chelm was. She felt like a girl, pressed against him from shoulder to thigh, and she smelled like a girl, and the sound of her breathing was the sound of a girl's breath. Grofield found himself getting interested despite himself and had to remind himself sternly that not only was this seeming girl in reality a priggish virgin who thought he was a crude kind of murderer; she and he were also in the middle of a desperate situation that offered no time off for dalliance.

Mind on business, Grofield. There's neither the time nor the place, and she isn't worth it anyway.

The voices outside receded, faded, ended. Grofield whispered, "Okay. I can't get at the knob."

"I've got it."

With light, Grofield's interest disappeared again. She was still the same tight-lipped, sexless wonder who'd come into the closet with him.

They had to wait at the door a minute; two of Danamato's men were strolling very slowly the length of the house. At last they made the far turn and went around it.

Grofield led the way now, moving fast and crouching, hoping no one was looking out an upstairs window. He wished he had time to dismantle the Mercedes, but it was impossible. They'd just have to get the hell out of here and hope for the best.

Grofield opened the passenger door of the Pontiac, flung the suitcase over the seat into the back, and slid across the seat to the steering wheel. The girl climbed in after him and shut the door. Loudly.

"Christ!" said Grofield. "Don't be so loud!"

"I'm sorry."

He snapped his fingers at her. "Give me the key."

She fumbled in a pocket of her skirt, but at last came up with a key ring. "It's the—"

"I know a GM key," he said, grabbed the ring, found the key with the hexagonal head, and put it in the ignition. "Where's your brother?"

"Roy?" she asked, turning her head to the back seat.

The answer came from the floor back there: "Here."

"Goody," said Grofield and turned the key in the ignition.

The Pontiac was shiftless. It started at once; he put it in drive and tromped on the accelerator, and they went tearing across the driveway toward the jungle.

In the rear-view mirror, Grofield saw people come running out the front door of the house. Then they were in the jungle growth, bucketing and careening down the narrow dirt road, and Roy Chelm was in the rear-view mirror instead.

"I'll try to make it to San Juan," Grofield said. "At least if we get out on the highway—"

"No," said Roy Chelm. "When you get down to the blacktop, turn right."

"That's the wrong way. We'll get up into the mountains, they'll pick us off easy."

"That's the way we're going," Chelm said.

"That Mercedes is a faster car than this," Grofield said. "They'll run us down."

"Do what I say," said Chelm.

"Go to hell," Grofield told him.

"Do as I say," repeated Chelm. And what could that cold thing against the side of Grofield's neck be but the barrel of a gun.

"God damn it," said Grofield wearily.

16

GROFIELD didn't slow for the turn at all. Foot clamped on the accelerator, he spun the wheel hard, and the Pontiac came roaring and bouncing and skidding out onto the black-top of 185 like a PT boat coming over a waterfall. An elderly Chevvy coming the other way nosed off into the ditch to avoid them, and Grofield kept spinning the wheel back and forth, keeping the Pontiac from lying over on its side the way it wanted to, until at last the car got its balance again and was willing to stay on all four wheels facing straight down the road. Then Grofield hunched grimly over the wheel, both hands gripping it high and tight, glaring through the windshield at the narrow, twisting blacktop road ahead of him, flanked tightly with jungle growth and jungle trees.

From the back seat Roy, his voice high and trembling, cried, "Are you trying to kill us?"

"I'm trying to keep us alive," Grofield snapped. He took a quick look in the mirror. The turn-off was still visible back there, and the Mercedes hadn't arrived yet. The Chevvy, out of the ditch, was moseying on again. With any luck the Mercedes would ram it and put itself out of commission.

Fat chance.

Grofield looked back at the road ahead, squealed through two bends, and the next time he checked the rear-view mirror the turn-off could no longer be seen. And still no Mercedes.

"You can slow down now," Roy said, his voice still too high.

"The hell I can," Grofield said.

"I have this gun pointed at your head, Mr. Grofield."

"That's nice. If you want to kill me while this car is doing seventy-five miles an hour, you just go ahead."

Beside him, Patricia Chelm twisted around in the seat and said to her brother, "Let him go, Roy. I think Mr. Grofield is good at this sort of thing."

"Thanks," said Grofield. Coming around a curve, he found an old Plymouth meandering along in the same direction, in the middle of the road. Grofield leaned on the horn, kept his speed up, and sliced through between the Plymouth and several tree trunks. There was a slight scraping sound on the right, where he kissed the Plymouth goodbye, and then they were past and tearing down the road again.

Still talking to her brother, Patricia Chelm said, "Why did you insist on coming this way? We want to get to San Juan, don't we?"

"They expect us to try to get to San Juan," Roy said. "If we went the way they expected, they'd catch up with us in no time. And remember, we have a murderer in the car with us. Danamato can even call the police in to help him."

"Intersection coming up," said Grofield.

You could go straight, or make a right. Both roads were black-top, similar, nothing to choose between them.

"Go straight," Roy said.

Grofield went straight. Two boys sitting on their heels beside the road at the intersection watched them go by, mouths open in surprise.

The road was twisting more and more, forcing Grofield to keep slamming on the brakes. He squealed around every curve, sometimes on the right side of the road and sometimes on the left. There was little traffic and what there was Grofield passed any which way, left or right, up or down, horn wailing, tires screaming, engine roaring.

Patricia Chelm kept being thrown into him, which was dangerous, and finally he snapped, "Don't you have a seat belt, for God's sake?"

"Why? Are you planning to have an accident?"

It was a remark he hadn't expected from her, and he wished he could take a look at her expression, but just now he was passing a slow-moving truck on a blind curve.

Once by it, he did look at her, but she had no expression at all. "What I want," he said, "is for you not to keep bouncing off my arm when I'm trying to steer. Tie yourself down."

"Oh. All right. I'm sorry."

The road was climbing. The jungle was more jungle, the little peasant shacks were fewer and fewer, the traffic was almost nonexistent now. Grofield said, "Where the hell have you got me?"

"Away from Danamato," said Roy.

"Maybe. Patricia, take a look in the glove compartment for a map."

She did, and said, "Here's one."

"Find out where we are."

"How? I never looked at one of these in my life."

"For God's sake! Chelm, what about you?"

"I'll try," he said doubtfully. "But I've never looked at one of them either."

"Oh, the hell with it!" Grofield stamped his foot onto the brake. The Pontiac slewed, slewed back, and shuddered to a stop. "Give me the map," he said, yanking it out of Patricia Chelm's hands. Then he saw the gun lying on the seat between them. That last braking had knocked Roy Chelm for a loop, punching him into the back of the front seat, popping the gun out of his hand so it fell on the front seat between his sister and Grofield, neither of whom had seen it till now.

They both saw it at the same second, but Grofield moved

faster. Patricia Chelm's nails dug into the back of his hand, and then he had the gun. "Well," he said and smiled at the gun. "Well, well, well."

Patricia Chelm watched him white-faced. "What are you going to do?"

From the back seat, Roy Chelm, pressing a handkerchief to a bloody nose, whispered, "You bastard."

"Everybody agrees on that," Grofield told him. "But I tell you what. You two manage not to get underfoot, I'll keep you with me as far as San Juan. You helped me back there at the Danamato house, so I owe you that. And since you let me get away, I don't think Danamato would treat you very nice if he caught up with you again."

"You'll take us along?" Patricia Chelm was almost whispering.

"Why not?" Grofield tucked the gun away under his left hip, where neither of them would be able to get at it, and opened the road map, saying, "Let's see where we are."

When he saw, he wasn't happy about it. Imagine the main road east from San Juan as a horizontal line, with a large letter U suspended from the middle of it. The left side of this letter U is route 185, the road Grofield had taken in from the highway when on his way to meet Belle Danamato in the first place. Farther down the U, route 185 branches off to the right, the intersection they'd already passed. After that, the road is numbered 186, and route 186 continues to the bottom of the U, makes the turn down there, and starts up the other side. And the other side of the U goes right through Sierra De Luquillo, the Luquillo Forest, which is a combination jungle and mountain range. Before getting back to that main highway, route 185 twists and turns through some of the wildest and least accessible country this side of a Tarzan movie. And the nicest part of it is, there aren't any other roads. That is, there are lots of side roads, all numbered nine hundred something, but they're all dead ends. The turnoff for 185, the one they'd already gone past, connected not much farther on with a main highway at Juncos, but 186 was a gauntlet with no way out except at the other end.

Grofield showed it to them, where they were and where they'd been and where they had to go.

Roy Chelm said, "Can't we go back to that turn-off?"

"How long do you think it'll take Danamato to get on our trail? All he has to do is ask a couple questions along the way. He's probably past that turn-off himself already."

Patricia Chelm said, "But what if he sends some of his men to the other end of this road? What if they're ahead of us, and he's behind us?"

"That's tough on us," Grofield said. He folded up the map and gave it back to her.

"What are we going to do?" she said.

"Bull through," he told her. "One way or the other. Hold on now." And he hit the accelerator again.

17

THEY ran out of gas in the middle of nowhere.

Grofield had checked the gauge when he'd first gotten into the car, and it had read half a tank. It still read half a tank, but the engine coughed twice on an upgrade, cut out near the peak, started again briefly as they crested, and quit for good as they started down the other side.

Grofield shifted into neutral and let gravity take over.

"What is it?" the girl asked. "Why's the engine stopped?"

"I'm not sure," he said. "It acts like we're out of gas, but the gauge shows half a tank."

"Could it be something else?"

"I don't know what."

From the back seat Roy Chelm said, "Pat, remember George talking about having to get something fixed on this car?"

She shook her head. "No."

"Over a week ago. Was it the gas gauge he said?"

"I don't remember it," she said. "I never listen to George anyway."

"You should have this time," Grofield told her.

They were well into the mountains now, dark green masses looming up on all sides, the road a narrow, twisting ribbon of black working its corkscrew way through the steep-sided tropical rain forest, called El Yunque, after its best-known mountain peak. Huge tree ferns hung over the road like a tumbledown green roof in the lower parts, keeping them in permanent shadow. Flamboyant trees crowded the blacktop on both sides, their roots coiled above the ground like gray snakes. On both sides the trees and vines and shrubs were all snarled together like an art-nouveau poster done in shades of green and black. Though it was noon and the sun was high in the sky, there was a moist coolness in the air, particularly in the lower parts of the road, a feeling like mildew, and here and there they'd passed narrow, tiny, furious waterfalls rushing down slick, glittering boulders.

This was a rain forest, and despite the high sun there was still a feeling of imminent rain. Eastward, thick black clouds like black pillows clumped around the mountaintops. It rained in this area nearly every day, and sometimes several times a day, sudden downpours that drenched quickly and moved on within minutes. To the east there was an experimental area, a controlled jungle operated by the United States Department of Agriculture. The main road through it, the road the tourists took, was three or four miles to the east, past the biggest mountains, El Yunque and El Toro and Monte Britton. Over there were activities and other people, a restaurant, places for the tourists to stop and take pictures. Over here on this road there was nothing. Not even a way to get over there.

Not even if there was gas in the car.

They hadn't seen another vehicle for a quarter of an hour, and they didn't see any now as they twisted and turned down the tortuous downgrade, Grofield letting the car roll as fast as he dared, hoping to get as much more mileage out of it as he could, hoping to get at least part way up the next hill before they'd have to get out and walk.

They rolled downhill in near silence, except for the shush of the wind of their passage, and all around them in the jungle they could hear the clicking and calling and crying of the jungle creatures, bugs and birds and beasts. It was like sailing in a glider, except when Grofield had to press down on the brake pedal and spin the wheel for them to squeal around another sharp curve.

There was the bottom, in darkness sufficient to cause Grofield to switch on the headlights. Massive trees, ripe with flat leaves and covered with vines, loomed up all around them. The road curved to the right, crossed a tiny bridge over a quick-flowing, minuscule stream, curved to the left, hit bottom, and curved upward and to the right.

Grofield took the curves with as little braking as possible, wanting speed, as much speed as he could get. The Pontiac nosed into the first up curve, seemed to sail along at the same pace for a few seconds, and then began to sag. The road straightened, then curved to the left again, getting steeper all the time. The car slowed more and more quickly, the speedometer needle dropping below thirty, below twenty, down toward ten.

There was a narrow break in the foliage on the left, a dirt road going in. Grofield spun the wheel hard; the Pontiac turned sluggishly, jounced off the road onto the dirt.

Patricia Chelm: "What are you doing?"

Roy Chelm: "Stop it!"

It wasn't really a road, just a little turn-around space poked into the jungle. Grofield kept the wheel tightly turned, pushed the Pontiac to the end of the cleared part, pushed deeper into vines and shrubs and bushes, and the car finally came to a stop about three lengths from the road.

Grofield switched off the ignition and the lights. A late-evening darkness settled on them.

Patricia Chelm said, "How are we going to get out of here?"

"We may have to walk," Grofield told her, "if no car shows up. We'll try hitchhiking first. If we're very, very lucky somebody will come along with an extra can of gas that they're willing to sell us."

Roy Chelm said, "Then why drive the car into the jungle?"

"Because you know who else might come along? Our friend

Danamato. I'd rather he didn't notice the car, because if he noticed the car he just might notice us."

"Oh," said Patricia.

"You two stay here," Grofield said. "I'll go stand at the road and wait for somebody to flag down."

He pushed open the car door and got out. It was chilly out here, cold and damp. He stuck his head back in the car window and said to Roy Chelm, "Get me a jacket out of my bag."

Chelm gave him one, and he put it on and walked back to the edge of the road. There was an old stone marker there, with nothing legible on it. Grofield sat on that, surrounded by dark-green chittering jungle, trees a mile high, an empty road curving away within feet in both directions.

"It's Alice in Wonderland," he told himself. "I must be the White Knight."

He shook his head in disgust, and watched no traffic go by.

18

GROFIELD opened the driver's door and slid in. "Take over for a while, Chelm," he said. "I'm cold and wet."

Chelm looked panicky. "Me? I don't know what to do."

"If you see a car," Grofield told him, "wave at it. Frantically. Try to look helpless and not like a madman or a murderer or a thief. Apparently that was my trouble—I don't look innocent enough."

Patricia Chelm said, "You mean that truck?"

He did. In the fifteen minutes he'd been out there—he stood most of that time, since the stone marker tended to make his butt cold—only one vehicle had passed, that a rickety old truck with a well-mustached, pop-eyed driver at the wheel and a lot of rusty automobile parts in the back. Grofield had waved at him to stop, and the truck had veered all over the road in the driver's frantic attempts to get around him and away from there. So much for the local Good Samaritans.

"Take fifteen minutes," Grofield told Chelm. "Then I'll take a turn again."

"Very well," Chelm said doubtfully. He got out on his sister's side of the car and Grofield watched him shamble round-shouldered out to the road and stand on the verge there, as de-jected as a character in a Beckett play.

Grofield shook his head and said to Patricia Chelm, "You two amaze me. I don't remember the last time I've seen two people so totally incapable of taking care of yourselves."

"We take care of ourselves," she said indignantly. "This is a special situation. Nobody would be expected to . . . You haven't done so well yourself, if it comes to that."

"I suppose not," Grofield said. He stretched his feet out be-tween the pedals and put his head back on the top of the seat. Closing his eyes, he said, "I'm tired. It's been a busy day, and I didn't get my eight hours last night."

They were both silent a minute and he was starting to doze off when she said, "Did you really kill Belle Danamato? You can tell me the truth."

Not moving, not bothering to open his eyes, he said, "The truth is no, I did not kill Belle Danamato."

"I believe you," she said. "I'm not sure why, but I do."

Grofield turned his head, opened one eye, and looked at her. "What about you?"

She didn't understand him. "Me?"

"Did you kill her?"

Her face got very cold and very angry. "Are you going to start that business again? The frigid virgin hiding inside her brother's pants?"

"That's a nice image," Grofield said. "Keep it in the act."

"I'm not acting!"

"But did you kill Belle Danamato, that's the question."

When she turned away and glared out the windshield in lieu of answering him, he closed his eye again, made his head more comfortable on the seat, and said, "Back there at the house, naturally part of what I was doing was trying to dazzle Dana-mato. But I was also interested in getting myself unframed by figuring out who really did do it. It had to be one of us bunnies upstairs, and so far as I can see, a motive of one kind or an-other can be made out on just about every one of us."

"Not me," she said thinly. "I may not have approved of Belle Danamato, but that doesn't mean I—"

"Ha hah!" He opened the eye again and grinned at her.

She met his gaze rigidly for a moment, then suddenly chuckled and looked away and said, "Oh, what the hell."

He raised his head, opened his other eye and said, "I beg your pardon?"

"I may not be quite as much the plaster saint as Roy thinks," she said, not looking at him. "Or as much as he wants." She looked back again, meeting his eye, her own expression more open now, more intent. "For God's sake, you saw Belle Danamato. Can you imagine her being engaged to a man she wasn't sleeping with?"

"No."

"Well, she thought it was the berries, believe me. Roy has that effect on people. He makes them want to be better than they are, makes them want to look good in his eyes."

"I hadn't noticed him affecting me that way," Grofield told her.

"It might be just with women," she said. "I've seen it happen time and time again. Roy *is* good, I mean morally good, whether he's physically weak or cowardly or not. That's another matter. He's morally good, he's much better than I am, but he makes me *want* to be good." She smiled crookedly, looking out the rear window in her brother's direction. "I'm the one around him most of the time," she said, "so naturally I'm the one who gets the fullest treatment. But . . ."

She'd stopped. Grofield looked at her and saw her eyes widening with shock. She was still looking toward the road.

Grofield spun around, looked out the rear window, and saw two men struggling with Roy. One was the bearded man, the other was one of the other of Danamato's men from the house. Just past them was a white Volvo, its doors standing open.

Grofield caught the movement from the corner of his eye, then caught the girl's hand just before it reached the door handle. Harshly he whispered, "What the hell are you doing?"

"Roy! We've got to stop them!"

"Are you crazy? There's two more in the car. Come on."

"Aren't we going to help Roy?" She couldn't believe it.

"Not by getting ourselves killed," he told her.

He turned the light switch on the Pontiac dash so the inside lights wouldn't go on when the door was opened, then quietly pushed open the door on his side and slid out. He gestured to her to follow him, and reluctantly she did, still looking back at where Roy struggled on the roadside with Danamato's men.

Three of them were holding him now, with only the driver left in the car. He was shouting, yelling, carrying on, and under the cover of all that noise and distraction Grofield and the girl managed to get away from the car and up the steep slope into the jungle growth.

Everything was wet in here, cold and wet and dark and dripping. The ground was slippery with clamminess; every branch and trunk they touched was cold and slimy to their hands. They struggled upward perhaps twenty feet, exhausting themselves in the process, and there Grofield called a halt. They sat on the wet ground, vines and leaves brushing their shoulders and arms, bushes crowding their feet, their backs against slimy tree trunks, and watched.

In the outside world it was still noontime, but here it was night, and it was only by the headlights of the Volvo that they could orient themselves. The Pontiac was a pale blur dimly seen through the greenery below them, and the struggle out by the road was simply indistinct motion, which soon ended.

"Silent now," Grofield whispered, and beside him, shivering, she nodded.

They heard the Pontiac being searched, doors opened and shut, then some scuffing in the nearby undergrowth as Danamato's men took a few steps in from the clearing; but the jungle was too dense, the possible directions of their escape too many, and the scuffing sounds soon ended. There was silence then for a few minutes, and finally the slamming of the Volvo doors and the sound of it driving away.

The girl started to move, but Grofield held her arm. "Let's wait awhile," he whispered.

She looked at him, her eyes very white in the near darkness. "Do you think they might?" she whispered.

"I would," Grofield whispered back. "I don't know if they would or not."

They waited ten minutes, but heard and saw no more movement. "All right," Grofield whispered finally. "We'll chance it. Let me go first."

"Of course," she whispered back, and when he looked at her in some surprise he saw a faint smile on her lips.

It did Patricia Chelm good, he decided, to get away from her brother every once in a while.

They were both stiff from staying so long in one position in such a cold and damp place. Grofield inched downward first, Roy Chelm's gun in his hand. It was quite a cannon, a 9mm Star Model A Super automatic, almost identical to the Colt Government automatic. Hit a man anywhere with a bullet from that gun and he'd spin around five times before going down. He would also stay down after he got there.

But there was no one in the vicinity of the Pontiac to shoot it at. They'd really gone, taking Roy Chelm with them.

Grofield looked in the back seat of the Pontiac, and his suitcase was still there. "Good," he said. "I'm changing out of this wet stuff. You got anything with you?"

"We put our luggage in the trunk before I went after you," she said.

Grofield laughed. "You two are something else," he said. He unlocked the trunk, and there were four suitcases. "Incredible," he said. "You got all this stuff in here without being seen."

"Mrs. Milford helped us," she said. "She kept watch for us, told us when the coast was clear."

"Mrs. Milford? She didn't strike me as the helpful type."

"She's really very nice when you get to know her," she said. "She's very unhappy, of course."

"Because of George."

"Naturally. Do you know he actually threw a pass at me? Me! Isn't that incredible?"

Grofield looked at her as though she were ugly. "Some people don't have any taste," he said. "They'll go after any pig in a skirt."

She almost said something angry, then she looked confused,

and finally she laughed. "You're very different from Roy," she said.

"I hope to Christ."

"I'm not used to anybody but Roy. I'm not used to the kind of responses I get from you."

"Me and George Milford," Grofield said.

"Oh, you wouldn't be like George," she said, as though she thought he'd been kidding.

"You mean I wouldn't throw a pass?"

"Not like *George*."

"What's the difference?"

"Well, he's so . . ." Abruptly, she blushed and turned away. "Never mind," she said. "We shouldn't be talking about this anyway."

"What should we be talking about?"

"What we're going to do now."

"That's easy," he said. "We're going to change clothes—you on this side of the car, me on that side—and then we're going to wait for somebody to give us a lift or some gas. And then we're going to San Juan."

"San Juan? But . . . won't Roy be back at the house?"

"Of course he will. But Danamato won't kill him. Danamato isn't a killer. He's a mobster, but he isn't a killer, not for spite. He'd kill me, because he thinks I killed his wife, but the worst he'll do to Roy is slap him around a little."

"Aren't you going to help save him?"

Grofield looked at her. For a while she would be useful, good camouflage. He'd prefer to have her cooperation. But when it came to climbing aboard old Rocinante and charging the Danamato windmill to rescue a feeble, useless buffoon like Roy Chelm, this girl was barking up the wrong Don. Not that he could tell her that, not yet, so he said, "Sure, I'll help save him. I'll do what I can. But first we've got to fall back and regroup. Get to San Juan, register in a hotel, get our—"

"Just a minute. What do you mean, register in a hotel?"

Grofield shook his head. "Honey, I'm not going to ask you to sacrifice your fair white body for my help in getting your brother back. We need a base of operations. I need a bath. We need sleep and food and time to think and work out a plan. You want to live in a tree?"

"All right," she said. "All right."

"Good. Let's change."

He started to brush by her, and she put a hand on his chest, looking up at him to say, "I'm sorry if I seem hypersensitive about sex. I do have a reason for it. I may tell you about it some day."

"Not the uncle who felt you up the Christmas you were six."

She blushed again and looked away. "No," she said. "Never mind, it doesn't matter."

So she was serious about it. She was one of those people who not only had a sexual hang-up; she knew she had a sexual hang-up and she knew what was causing the sexual hang-up and she relished going over and over it in her head, like a little boy telling a dirty story.

Not getting there is half the fun.

Grofield shook his head and went around to the other side of the car and changed into dry clothes. He knew she was also changing, just across the way, and he really didn't give a damn.

19

THE bellboy left with a Grofield dollar clenched in his fist, and Grofield went over to look out at Ashford Avenue, the main tourist street of San Juan, lined with hotels imported from Miami Beach. Because they didn't have a reservation, but had been trying hotels looking for one with an unfilled cancellation, they didn't have an ocean-view room, but Grofield didn't much care whether he ever saw the ocean again or not. What the room did look out on was the curving-drive entrance to the hotel, four stories down, with the fountain splashing in the middle, lit by spotlights of varied colors. Automobiles moved from left to right along Ashford, a one-way street, but there were practically no pedestrians.

A sigh of contentment made him turn around, to see Patricia Chelm lying spread-eagled on one of the double beds, smiling blissfully up at the ceiling. "A bed," she murmured. "Never in my life have I been so happy to be in a bed."

"I believe it," Grofield said.

She either didn't hear him or didn't understand him. Tucking her chin in sufficiently so she could see him she said, "I know I shouldn't be enjoying myself like this, with God knows what happening to Roy, but I can't help it. This is heaven!"

"Enjoy enjoy," Grofield said. "Why should Roy begrudge you a little rest and relaxation? You've earned it."

They both had. They'd waited another two hours in the dank darkness of the rain forest—and in fact sat huddled together in the Pontiac during one brief torrential downpour—before at last a car came along, with some sort of American engineer in it. He was headed for San Juan, too, and he had a jerry can of gas in the trunk. "You got to have extra gas around this joint," he said seventy times. "You get off the main roads, they's no stations worth shit."

Grofield had gotten the Pontiac started up, and he followed the engineer out to the main highway and a gas station, where he filled both the Pontiac and his rescuer's jerry can. It was late afternoon by then, and it was later afternoon by the time they reached San Juan and started trying the hotels. San Juan hotels tend to be booked several weeks in advance, so this was the fifth hotel they'd tried, and here the desk clerk kept telling them how much luck they were in. "You folks are sure in luck," he'd say and shake his head in awe. Grofield signed in as Mr. and Mrs. Alex Dann from New York City, the bellboy carried his one suitcase and the girl's two, and now at last they could sit down and relax a minute.

She was already doing it, and Grofield joined her, dropping onto the other bed and kicking off his shoes. "In a little while," he said, "we better go get some dinner. You ever been to Mallorquina?"

"No. What is it?"

"A restaurant up in the old town. Later."

"Much later," she said.

Grofield looked over at her, but all she'd meant was rest. He shook his head and closed his eyes.

There was silence for a few minutes, and Grofield was almost asleep when she said, "When are we going after Roy?"

"Tomorrow," he said. "There's nothing we can do any more

today. We'll get a good night's sleep and start out in the morning."

"All right," she said.

There was silence again, and she broke it again, this time saying, "One thing I ought to mention."

He'd been almost asleep again. "What?" he said in some irritation, his eyes squeezed shut.

"Just in case you were thinking of ditching me tomorrow," she said. "I ought to tell you what I'd do in such a case. I'd call the police at once, I'd give them the full story, I'd insist you *were* the murderer. They'd go out to the house and maybe Roy would get killed or injured, maybe he wouldn't. But one thing I know for sure: you wouldn't get on a plane. You wouldn't get off this island. There wouldn't be Mr. Danamato with half a dozen men looking for you, there'd be the whole police force looking for you."

Grofield opened his eyes and looking at the ceiling. His look was bitter.

"Just so you understand," she said.

"I think I do," Grofield said. "I think I understand."

20

SEVEN.

The croupier pulled the dice on with the stick, pulled the shooter's chips in—"He fails to make his point"—and pushed the dice toward Grofield, next along the table.

Grofield picked them up, turned them between his fingers, looked at them, and held them up to Patricia Chelm. "Blow on them for luck," he said.

They'd had wine with dinner, and she was a little high. She smiled a lopsided smile of embarrassment and said, "Should I?"

"Certainly."

"Hah!" she said on the dice, and Grofield flipped them at the backboard.

"Eleven!" announced the croupier, and where two twenty-dollar chips had been there were now four. Grofield left them there, held the dice up to the girl again and said, "Once more."

"Hah!"

He flipped.

"Six! The point is six. The shooter's point is six, his point is six."

The dice came back, and Grofield picked them up again.

She whispered, "Again?"

"We'll ride on the luck," he told her. "Won't need another shot of it till we make the point this time." He flipped the dice and bought a ten.

It was a little after eleven at night and they were in the ground-floor casino of their hotel. Gambling was legal here in Puerto Rico, but the casinos here didn't have the desperate, greedy urgency of Las Vegas, where the gambling rooms have neither clocks nor windows to remind the fish of the passing of time. In San Juan the casinos are merely entertainment appendages of the tourist industry, along with the beaches and the floor shows and the trips to St. Thomas for the duty-free liquor. They are open only eight hours a day, from eight in the evening until four in the morning, and only three kinds of gambling are available for the idle speculator: roulette, blackjack, craps.

They'd wandered in here after coming back from Old San Juan, where they'd had dinner in Mallorquina, an old restaurant on one of the narrow, steep side streets out near Castle Morro. The restaurant was ancient, functional, high-ceilinged, white everywhere, from white tile floor through white table-cloths to white walls and ceiling. A heavy, dark wood bar ran along one side. Large broad doors stood open onto the slanting street, well lit against the night, where tourists and natives crowded along the narrow strip of sidewalk between the parked cars and the building front.

There'd been a tropical rainstorm while they were there, the street turning suddenly gray with vertical sheets of rain. Half a dozen pedestrians had ducked through the open doorways into the restaurant, standing just back from the curtain of rain, grinning at one another and talking with the waiters. Then the rain stopped, as abruptly as it had started, leaving the automobile hoods gleaming in the streetlights. The pedestrians moved on, a cool breeze entered the restaurant from the street, and it became again possible to attract the attention of a waiter.

In the month she'd been here, it turned out Patricia Chelm had seen practically nothing of Puerto Rico except the airport and Belle Danamato's house, so after dinner they wandered around the old town for a while, then drove slowly back to the hotel, winding up at last here in the hotel casino, where she had watched the roulette with fascination for a while, the blackjack with bewilderment for a while, and finally the crap table, where Grofield made his six on the fourth role but failed to make his next point, a five, sevening out on the third role instead.

"That's enough for me," he said. "Come along, Patricia, we've got to get up early in the morning."

"Pat," she said.

"What?"

"I hate Patricia," she said. "I wish somebody on this stinking earth would call me Pat."

"Pat," Grofield said, "are you snockered?"

"All I had was wine," she said. "And that sangria stuff."

"That was wine, too."

"Right. And a couple of drinks at the bar, remember?"

"I remember."

"I may be a little high," she said, "but I'm not snockered."

"That's good," he said.

They went upstairs and she stood in the middle of the room looking at the beds. "How do we work this? You hang blankets up like Clark Gable?"

"No," he said. "I go to bed in my underwear, and we turn the lights out and we say good night. Very simple."

"Oh." She looked at him, and she *was* high. "I'm not a virgin really, you know."

"You're not?" What he was, mostly, was tired. He really wasn't in the mood for her flickering flame right now.

"There was one man," she said bitterly.

"Oh," said Grofield. "The awful experience, right?"

"It's easy for you to sneer," she said.

"Well, I've practiced."

"I'll tell you about him," she said. "Then see if you want to sneer."

He sat down on the bed, crossed his legs, and parodied attentiveness. "I'm all ears," he said.

"You're a bastard," she told him.

"So everybody says."

"But not as big a bastard as Jeff."

"Jeff."

"He was married," she said dramatically. "He didn't tell me —till it was too late."

"Oh, for Christ's sake," said Grofield.

"He got me pregnant." Her tone was flat now, the words like stones dropped into the room. "I had an abortion. I was seventeen."

She meant Look-how-young-I-was, but Grofield didn't take it that way. "You're twenty-two now, aren't you?" he said.

"Yes."

"Isn't it time you got over it?"

She blinked at him. She shook her head. She said, "Roy doesn't talk to me like that."

"Roy likes you dependent on him," Grofield said. "That way he can go on depending on you."

"That doesn't make any sense."

"Sure it does. You're a couple of emotional cripples leaning on each other."

"Emotional cripples! What a rotten thing to say!"

"It's the truth," Grofield told her, too tired to give a damn. "Your mind is girdled up tighter than Eva Milford's ass."

"Hah!" she said, and when Grofield looked up she was laughing. She went on laughing.

"You're stoned," he told her.

She stopped laughing. She said, "I am not. I'll admit I'm high, I've had enough to relax me, but I'm not stoned. And when are you going to kiss me?"

"I'm not," Grofield said.

"Why not? George Milford thought I was hot stuff."

Grofield laughed and got up off the bed and put his arms around her.

A little later, as he was reaching for the light switch, she looked up at him and whispered, "For the love of God, don't get me pregnant. All right?"

"Count on it," Grofield promised.

21

"GROFIELD," she said, and he woke up.

He opened his eyes, and she was up on one elbow beside him, looking down at him. Past her head he could see light pouring through the windows, it was morning, they were both in the same bed.

"Call me Alan," he said lazily, and stretched and put his hands on her shoulders.

She pulled back, saying, "The car, Alan! They'll look for the car!"

"Of course they will," he said cheerfully. "Give us a good-morning kiss, ducks."

But she wouldn't be drawn down. "They'll go back to where we were stranded," she said urgently. "They'll see the car gone, they'll know we still have it with us. Won't they think to look in the hotel garages?"

"Definitely," he said, smiling up at her. "Good thinking. If I was Danamato, I'd send somebody up and down Ashford first thing this morning, tell him to look in all the hotel garages, see if he sees the Pontiac around the neighborhood somewhere."

"Well, he *will!* It's downstairs!"

"Of course it is," said Grofield. "Patricia, I require your warm and willing lips."

"But . . ." She kept pulling away from him, tense and urgent, for a few seconds more, then suddenly stopped, planted a hand on his chest and said suspiciously, "You already knew it."

"Of course."

"You knew it last night."

Smiling, he touched a fingertip to her nose. "One hundred per cent," he said.

"Why? For heaven's sake, do you *want* them to find us?"

"Me," Grofield said. "Yes, I do, I want them to find me."

"And that's why we went out last night? Out to the restaurant, and sightseeing, and into the casino. So people could see us."

"That was one of the reasons," he said. "Not the only one, or I would have gone by myself."

She shook her head, frowning at him. "I don't understand," she said. "We worked so hard to get *away* from them."

"If you will recall," Grofield said, "you have a brother named Roy. I am under orders from you either to return that brother or have you blow a very loud whistle on me."

"So?"

"So how many men does Danamato have? About half a dozen down here? Maybe more, maybe eight. Let's say eight. Plus himself, of course. So say nine. Nine armed men, all between me and your brother. Do I want all nine of them sitting around the house out there, where they could cause me trouble? No, I do not. I want some of them in one place, and some of them in another place, and some of them yet someplace else. I want Danamato's troops diversified, and the only way I can get them diversified is to let them chase me around awhile."

"What if they catch us?"

"Me," Grofield corrected. "And I'd rather they didn't, so I'll do my best to avoid it."

"*Us,*" she said. "You're not going anywhere without me."

"Nonsense," Grofield said. "I'll have to move fast. I—"

"I can move fast. And we're staying together."

She seemed very determined. Grofield said, "Pat, I'm thinking about your safety. This isn't going to be too simple, you know."

"Maybe you are," she said. "And maybe you're thinking of hightailing it out to the airport and taking the next plane for anywhere. I'll stay with you, Alan, until Roy is free."

Grofield looked shocked. "You don't trust me?"

"Not for a second," she said.

"Honey, I can't—"

"Honey, you have to." She bent quickly, brushed his lips with hers, and started out of bed, saying briskly, "Now, we'd better—"

"Whoa, there!" He grabbed her arm and pulled her back. "Let's go through that last part again, with a little more feeling."

She wound up lying across his chest, her face just above his. Smiling down at him, she said, "We're staying together, aren't we?"

"Until the end, my love," he promised.

"Good." She lowered her head and kissed him, this time more emphatically.

"Mmm," he said. "Tell me. When we get Roy back, do you intend to revert to the old style?"

"Old-style what?"

"You know what I mean."

She nibbled his ear. "I don't know what you're talking about," she murmured. "Haven't I always been like this?"

"Of course," he said. He nuzzled her neck.

"Shouldn't we be starting?" she asked, though not with much urgency.

"It's early yet," Grofield assured her, not having any idea what time it was. "They might not even have found the car yet."

"Oh."

"We want to give them plenty of chance to find it and get set."

"That makes sense," she whispered.

"So we can take our time," he said softly, rolling her over.

"That's good," she said, and smiled, and closed her eyes.

22

GROFIELD stood by the window, looking out at Ashford Avenue and tucking his shirt in. Room service had just delivered breakfast, steaming on the small table just to his right. It was a little after ten o'clock, and in this air-conditioned room it was hard to believe that the glaring, sunny world just the other side of that glass was probably twenty degrees hotter and three times as humid as the air in here.

Pat came out of the bathroom, dressed and made up. She was smiling this morning, and the smile softened her features, made them seem less bony and hard. Her body seemed to have a new softness today, too, added softness without added weight. She'd tied her hair with a pale-blue ribbon at the base of her neck, and that improved her appearance, too.

"Breakfast!" she exclaimed. "I could eat a horse."

"Come here a second," he said. When she did, he pointed out the window. "See that?"

"The Mercedes!"

The black car was parked illegally directly across the street from the hotel, between a dress boutique and a budget car-rental agency.

"There's someone at the wheel," Grofield said. "That puts one or two in the garage down in the basement. They'll try to grab us when we go down there."

"So what do we do?"

"We don't go down." Grofield shook his head. "I wish you trusted me out of your sight."

"Why?"

"I'd have you take off in the Pontiac while I went across there and rented a car. That would take a couple out of the play right away, and give me better odds."

"But I don't drive," she said.

Grofield looked disgusted. "What I should do," he told her, "is knock you out, tie you up, and leave you in the closet."

"Why don't you?"

He shrugged. "I'm a sucker, I suppose."

"You're not sure it would give you enough time," she said, "that's what you mean. The only way you could feel safe from me is if you killed me, and that much of a rat you're not."

"You give me too much credit," Grofield said.

She laughed and said, "Come eat your breakfast before it gets cold." She sat down and reached for orange juice.

Grofield stayed a minute longer at the window. "I don't see the Volvo anywhere," he said.

"Volvo?" She took a bite of toast.

"White Volvo," he said. "The one that took Roy away." He turned away from the window and sat down at her right.

"I didn't see it well enough," she said. "It was a Volvo? Where do you think it is?"

"I *hope* it's at the airport," Grofield said. "Danamato won't expect me to do anything but try to get off the island. So he should have a couple of boys waiting out at the airport. Just in case I slip past the ones around the hotel."

She shivered. "I'm glad they didn't try to get in here last night."

"Why should they? All they'd do would be attract attention

to themselves, cause a ruckus in the hotel, get the law looking this way." Grofield grinned bleakly. "Danamato doesn't want the law to get me for killing his wife, he wants to take care of me himself."

"If only," Pat said, "we could figure out who really did kill Belle."

"I know who killed her," Grofield said, picking up his orange juice. "It doesn't make any difference." He drank the juice.

She stared at him. "You know?"

"Yes." Grofield attacked his eggs.

"Well?" she said.

He looked at her. "Oh, no," he said. "Tell you, you mean? Not a chance of it."

"For heaven's sake, why not?"

He swallowed egg, sipped coffee, put the cup back down. "Because," he said, "you won't believe me. I'll say the name, you'll say but it couldn't be, I'll say but it is, you'll say what makes you think that, I'll get into a whole thing defending myself, trying to prove it . . ." He shook his head. "I'm not going to get involved in that," he said. "I have too many other things to think about." He ate some toast.

She stared at him in disbelief. "Are you joking with me? Is this some sort of gag?"

"No," he said. "Quiet, now, I'm thinking."

"What do you mean, be quiet? Do you really and truly know who killed Belle?"

"Yes," he said around a mouthful of egg. "I wish I could be sure that Volvo was out at the airport. Too bad we can't go out there and take a look for ourselves."

"Why don't you tell Danamato?" she said. "Just go tell him this person is the killer."

Grofield looked at her. "That would be smart," he said. "That would be brilliant."

"What's wrong with it?"

"Do you think," Grofield asked her, "Danamato would take my word for it? Honey, *you* wouldn't take my word for it."

"Try me."

"No. And I won't try Danamato either."

She frowned. She poked her fork at her eggs a minute. Looking at the eggs, she said, "Don't you have any proof?"

"Not a bit. Not a fingerprint, not a tire mark, not a mysterious letter in the culprit's handwriting, nothing."

She shook her head. "Then you can't be absolutely sure, can you?" she said.

He grinned and pointed his toast at her. "There," he said. "You disbelieve me without even hearing the name."

"But you *can't* be sure."

"All right, I can't." He popped the last of the toast in his mouth and finished his coffee. "You ready?"

She studied him critically. "I never know when you're lying," she said.

"Always," he told her. He got to his feet, went to the phone, got the desk and asked for a bellboy.

She said, "What do we want a bellboy for?"

"We give him the car keys, we have the car brought around to the front of the hotel. We don't go down into the garage."

"Oh," she said. "All right. That makes sense."

"Thank you." He went over and looked out the window, and the black Mercedes-Benz was still there. As he watched, a guy in a pale-gray suit walked down the hotel drive and across the street and got into the Mercedes on the passenger side. The car didn't go anywhere.

Behind Grofield, Pat said, "Sometimes you can be infuriating, you know it?"

"Come here," he said.

"I think you're lying," she said. "I think you don't know a thing, you're just playing games with me, having fun at my expense."

"Come here!"

She heard the seriousness in his tone and came over to the window, saying, "What's the matter?"

"Watch the Mercedes," he said. "There'll be a guy getting out of it in a minute."

She turned her head and watched the Mercedes. "What guy?" she said.

"You tell me."

They stood there a minute, both watching, and then the passenger door opened again and the guy got out. Ashford is one-way, but he looked both ways before crossing the street and coming back up the hotel driveway.

"That's one of them!" she said.

"He was at the house."

"Yes. When you and Danamato were questioning people one at a time, he and another man were guarding us in the other room."

Grofield nodded. "I hadn't seen him before," he said. "I was wondering if Danamato had brought in fresh troops this morning. He shouldn't. I'm only one man and this is an island." He turned away from the window. "Where the hell's the bellboy?"

"You're nervous," she said.

He looked at her in surprise. "Of course I'm nervous. I'm nervous every time I go up against nine men with guns. Who wouldn't be nervous?"

She smiled and said, "I'm sorry, I guess I just think of you as very competent."

"I am very competent," he told her. "I am also nervous. The two are not incompatible."

"All right."

He walked around the room, thinking things over. He had a smallish idea of a plan, an outline for a plan, but there was still a lot of it he was going to have to improvise as he went along. He didn't like that; he liked his scripts solid and dependable.

"Is it Marba?"

He looked at her in some annoyance, displeased at the interruption. "What?"

"Is the killer Marba?" she said.

"Cut it out," he said, and turned his back on her, and walked around the room some more.

23

P A T twisted around and looked out the back window. "They're about seven cars back," she said.

"Still no white Volvo?"

"Nothing white at all," she said.

They were on route 3 again, the road he'd taken from the airport the day before yesterday—two days ago, incredible! —and it was still just as crowded, with the same endless line of traffic meandering through the gentle curves eastward from San Juan. In fact, so far as Grofield could see it wasn't just the same traffic, it was the same individual cars. The same red rusting Chevvy, the same yellow-and-blue Ford station wagon, the same black Okie truck, and in the rear-view mirror the same black Mercedes-Benz, occasionally managing to shoot out and pass a car.

"Six," she said.

"I saw it," he told her, and looked front again. He was behind a bus himself right now, a blue belcher waddling down the road with its rear windows piled high with wicker baskets.

He practically had to get into the left lane to see if there was any traffic coming in that lane, and there usually was, so unless the Mercedes got within two or three cars Grofield planned on staying right where he was.

They hadn't come down from the hotel room, he and Pat, until the desk had called to say their car was waiting for them at the front door, and then they moved with smooth and unobtrusive speed, out of the elevator and across the lobby and out to the humid and sun-bright day outside.

Unfortunately, the smiling mustached young man who'd brought the car around was still in it, behind the wheel, ostentatiously emptying the ashtray and failing to get it back into the dashboard. In the meantime, Danamato's man, the one they'd seen from the window coming back to the hotel, had gotten out of his chair in the lobby, had walked out of the hotel and seen the two of them trying to get into the Pontiac, and had trotted away toward the Mercedes.

The smiling mustached young man just kept poking the ashtray at the dashboard until Grofield reached in and took him by the arm and tugged him out of there. He plucked the ashtray from the smiling young man's hand and threw it into the fountain. Then he got behind the wheel—Pat was already in on the other side—and they drove away from there, leaving the mustached young man looking after them with a bewildered smile on his helpful face.

But it had taken too long. They didn't have one man in the Mercedes following them now; they had two.

Hadn't there been anyone waiting for them in the garage in the basement? Grofield kept watch in the mirror as much as he could, and Pat stayed turned around in the seat for the first twenty minutes, but they saw no other car come out of the hotel after them, nor did any car except the Mercedes seem to follow them through all the turns and reversals Grofield made in the course of getting out of San Juan.

But there had to have been a couple of them down there; it only made sense. And they had to have seen the Pontiac driven out by the hotel employee. Why hadn't they followed it?

Grofield finally decided they'd figured the moving of the

Pontiac was a dodge to get them out of the basement, so Grofield and Pat could go down through the basement and slip away without being seen. In any case, they had to consider that a possibility. So there were only two on his immediate trail. Take them out and the odds would be improved, if only slightly.

"Five," Pat said, and Grofield looked into the mirror in time to see the Mercedes cut back in after having passed one more car.

"That's nice," Grofield said, and ahead of him the bus started applying various sets of brakes. It was signaling for a right, but it wasn't making a right; it was just going more and more slowly, wheezing gradually to a stop, swaying slightly on its springs.

Loiza was coming up and the turn-off to the house. It was there the bus was planning to stop, finally pulling off the road when it got down to ten miles an hour. Grofield shot around it, not quite grazing a truck coming the other way, and roared past the intersection, accelerating toward the next car in line, a vintage Plymouth painted lavender. When he got close enough he could see the brushmarks.

Pat cried, "Hey, that was the turn!"

"We've got plenty to do before we go in there," Grofield told her. There was a little clear road ahead, perhaps enough. Grofield goosed the Pontiac out around the lavender Plymouth. There was a car coming, appearing from around the next curve, but let *him* hit the brakes.

He did. Grofield cut between him and the Plymouth, and was now behind a Volkswagen Microbus.

Pat was looking at him suspiciously. "You aren't trying to pull something funny, are you?"

"Talk sense," he said. "We've got to get rid of those boys behind us before we do anything else."

She looked at the Mercedes, then back at Grofield. "You mean lose them?"

"I mean take them out of the play."

She looked startled. "How?"

"Effectively," he said.

"You don't . . . you aren't going to kill them, are you?"

"I'll tell you later," he said.

"No, wait!" She sat around right in the seat beside him, facing him, expression worried. "I don't want anybody to get killed," she said. "I don't want anybody to kill you, and I don't want you to kill anybody else."

"I agree with you," he said. "And I hope it works out that way."

"But it might not?"

"It might not." He glanced at her, her worried face and wide eyes, then looked back at the road. "You knew that, didn't you? What did you think was going on?"

"I don't want you to kill anybody!"

"You want me to get Roy for you, don't you?"

"Yes, of course!"

"The guys around him don't want Roy to get away," Grofield said. "In fact, they don't want *me* to get away. And they're all heeled. You know? Heeled. Carrying guns."

"I know what it means."

"Do you?"

She opened her mouth, then shut it again, and now she looked very troubled. She shook her head, looked back at the Mercedes, looked at Grofield's face again, shook her head once more. "I don't know what to say," she said. "I don't want anybody to get killed."

"It's up to you," Grofield told her. "I'm willing to turn around right now, spend a few minutes dusting these guys off our tail, go to the airport and take the next plane out of here. Sooner or later Danamato will probably let your brother go."

"He will not," she said. "You know that as well as I do. If you get away for good, he'll kill Roy in your place. Because Roy helped you escape, and because Roy was going to marry Belle, and just because that's the kind of man Danamato is."

Grofield shrugged. "Maybe," he said. "But I'll tell you the kind of man I am. If I'm going up against half a dozen armed men who are prepared to kill me, I figure I'm crazy if I'm not prepared to kill them. I may not be in a hurry to, maybe I'd rather not, but I've got to be ready to do it or I might just as well jump off a cliff and be done with it."

"Why can't you—what did you say?—dust these guys off your tail now, and let it go at that? Why do you have to kill them?"

"I didn't say kill them, I said take them out of the play. If I can do it without anybody getting hurt, so much the better."

"But why do it at all?" she insisted. "Why not just lose them?"

"Because," Grofield told her, "then they'll go back to the house for further orders. They'll be at the house when we get there, and they'll make the odds worse."

"Oh," she said.

"I'm counting on getting rid of these two," he said. "I'm counting on two more being at the airport, to cover me in case I get away from these two behind me. If there was anybody in the hotel garage, and there probably was, they've probably gone on back to the house, and there's nothing I can do about that. That puts probably four men at the house when we get there, with one or two down by the road and the others inside. Plus Danamato. Those odds are bad enough. I don't want them any worse."

"Of course not," she said.

Grofield glanced at the speedometer. They'd come eight miles since Loiza; the turn he wanted should be coming up any minute.

She said, "It seemed simple at first. Roy was caught, you could get him back. Now I don't know."

"It's still simple," he told her. "You want your brother back, or you want to avoid trouble?" He glanced at her and grinned. "Frankly, I think you do a hell of a lot better without Roy anyway."

She smiled back despite herself, saying, "Don't talk like that. This is serious."

"That it is," Grofield said. The traffic was thinning out somewhat, and in the rear-view mirror he saw that the Mercedes was only four cars back. As he watched it came shooting around number four and now it was only three cars back.

And here was the turn. Route 191, the scenic route through the rain forest. Grofield had seen no other cars make the turn ahead of him. He accelerated into it, and shot away from route 3, trying to get as much distance between himself and the Mercedes as he could. He knew this road from previous times on Puerto Rico, knew it wound and curved around even more than the one they'd been on yesterday, which would cut down the Mercedes' advantage of speed, but in the first mile or so the road was fairly level and straight, and it was on this stretch that the Mercedes stood the best chance of catching up with him and forcing him off the road.

She was facing back again, staring down the road toward route 3. "Here they come!"

He saw them in the mirror. No other cars in the way now. The rain forest wasn't that popular a tourist attraction, so that even at the height of the season there was sometimes ten or fifteen minutes between cars traveling the nineteen miles from one end of the road to the other.

The mountains loomed ahead; the air was already a bit cooler. And the Mercedes was gaining, slowly but steadily.

Pat pounded the top of the seat. "Faster! Faster!"

"Tell General Motors."

There was a big old farm truck coming, the kind used for carrying sugar cane stalks to be burned. This one was empty, and rattling, and moseying along. Grofield started twisting the wheel back and forth as he bore down on the truck, blaring his horn and careening from side to side of the road, then finally staying on the left, flashing his headlights, leaning on the horn, demanding the left side, and at the last minute the driver of the truck, terrified and astonished, spun the wheel and goosed the truck onto the wrong side of the road.

"My God!" shrieked Pat, and they chipped a rear reflector off the truck as they snaked through.

Pat, her hands to her head, her eyes round with shock, screamed, "What was *that* for?"

"Look," Grofield told her.

She turned around and looked. The truck was angled across the road. The Mercedes couldn't be seen at all.

"You did it!" she cried, jumping up and down for joy.

Grofield tapped the brakes, slowing slightly.

She looked at him in amazement. "What are you slowing down for?"

"I don't want to lose them, I just want to keep them from catching up. Can you see them? Did they hit the truck?"

"No. The truck's getting out of the way. They're in the ditch. They're backing out."

"All right," Grofield said, and leaned on the accelerator again. He said, "You make up your mind?"

She'd been shocked out of her former train of thought. "About what?" she said.

"Whether you want me to go through with this or not."

"Oh. Yes, I do. If somebody's going to get killed, I don't want it to be Roy." She put a hand on his arm. "Or you."

"I'll do my best," he promised. "I'm going to need your help. You willing?"

"Of course."

"All right. There's five or six places we could stop and set things up for them. We'll pick whichever one doesn't have any tourists at it. But we'll have to have an idea what we're going to do at any one of them."

She sat around in the seat again, facing him, hands in her lap. "Tell me what to do," she said.

$$24$$

"Is it Mrs. Milford?"

He looked at her. "Is what Mrs. Milford?"

"The killer," she said.

He faced the road again. "I'm sorry I said anything at all," he said. "Just lay off about that."

This was a good day on this road, with very few tourists, though so far there'd been just enough to be troublesome. There were two spots Grofield had had in mind as possible, but there had been one car stopped at each of them. In addition to those two, he'd passed one other car traveling in his direction and met three coming the other way in the ten minutes since the road had started to climb.

There was no way to make any time on this road. Pushing very hard and running into no other traffic at all, a man might average a little better than thirty miles an hour here. Whether he was driving a Pontiac or a Mercedes-Benz.

Grofield hadn't seen the black Mercedes since the road had

entered the rain forest, but he was sure it was still back there. This road went nowhere but to the rain forest and through it and out the other side, finally meeting route 31 between Naguabo and Juncos.

The eight-kilometer marker had just gone by, so that meant the next possible place was just ahead. This one Grofield thought the least likely, because it was the most popular with tourists.

No. There it was, and no cars were parked there at all.

"What's that?" Pat said, staring at it.

Grofield grinned. "That's our spot," he said.

Ahead of them, at the peak of a climbing right-hand curve, was a blue-gray tower straight out of Camelot, complete with the squared-off sawtooth fortress wall around the top. An observation tower, it was about forty feet high, with nothing inside but a circular staircase going up to the top, from which, on a clear day, it was possible to see as far as the Virgin Islands.

There was a small empty parking area in front of the tower. Grofield nosed the Pontiac in there, cut the ignition, pocketed the key, and they both got out.

It was going to rain soon, despite the blue sky directly overhead and the late-morning sun beaming down from the east. There was the smell of rain in the air, sharp and cool and moist. On the rising mountainside across the road all the tree leaves had turned upside down, showing a pale grayish green swath across the landscape, as though this one mountain out of all the mountains here had been faded by the sun. A notice near the entrance to the tower said that when those leaves were turned over like that it meant there would soon be rain, but with the smell of it in the air they didn't need leaves to tell them.

The rain clouds were to the south, dark and heavy, clumped around the mountaintops. To the east and north, the choked valleys were dim and green and dank with vegetation, and far beyond them Grofield could see the ocean, flat and blue, and the narrow tan line of shore between the blue and the green.

"Good luck to us," Grofield said, and started toward the tower.

"Alan," she said.

He stopped and looked back at her. "You're right," he said, and walked back and put his arms around her and kissed her.

"Now good luck to us," she said.

"Right." He touched her cheek and turned away.

There was damn little time. He trotted into the tower and up the cream-colored steps. At intervals there were glassless arched window openings in the outer wall, about three feet high and a foot and a half wide. Grofield stopped at the first of these through which he could see the road and the parking area. He sat on the steps so he could look out without being seen and waited with the automatic in his lap. Pat, he knew, was just outside the tower entrance, about fifteen feet below him, waiting for them to arrive.

It wasn't long. Less than a minute went by and there was the Mercedes, curving up and into sight, suddenly turning hard and jumping toward the parking lot, squealing to a stop beside the Pontiac.

Pat should now be out of sight. She was supposed to have waited till she knew they'd seen her, then to have run into the tower as though having arrived here just barely ahead of the Mercedes.

The two in the Mercedes now had a choice. They could either stay cautiously inside their car and wait to see what happened next or, excited by having just seen the rabbit duck into the hole, they could come running, planning to get out of target range and into the tower before Grofield could get set. The fact that tourists might show up at any second from either direction should help to pressure them toward making a move.

Yes. The Mercedes had barely rocked to a halt when both doors popped open and the two of them dashed out. One was the guy who'd been stationed in the hotel lobby this morning, and the other one was Jack. Both had guns in their hands as they came running down the cement walk from the parking area to the tower.

Grofield let them get about halfway and then he fired a shot out the window toward the valley to the right.

Grass flanked the cement walk on both sides, and the two

men reacted right, hitting the grass in two directions, Jack diving to the right and the other one to the left.

But there was nowhere for them to go, no cover to get behind. They were in the open, without a chance to do anything about it, and they had to know that if they were the pros Grofield thought they were.

Grofield shouted, "Stay there, or the next one's a hit!"

Jack stopped rolling and stayed where he was, on his stomach, arms out in front of him, but the other one kept rolling away to the left, trying to get out of Grofield's sightline. Grofield took aim and dropped a bullet in the area of the guy's knees. The guy shouted, came part way up off the ground, dropped back down, and rolled over on his back. He didn't move.

From down below, Pat screamed, "No! Alan, no!"

Grofield stuck his head out and saw her come rushing out the tower entrance. "Get the hell back!" he shouted, but she paid no attention, so he switched his own attention to Jack, shouting, "Jack, don't move or you're a dead man!"

"I hear you!" Jack shouted back, his voice muffled a bit because his face was in the grass.

Grofield yelled at Pat, "Come back here! I hit him in the leg!"

But she'd reached him by now. She dropped to her knees beside him, and Grofield cursed her at the top of his lungs. Now the guy would grab her, use her as a shield, force Grofield to surrender in return for the idiot girl's life, and he wasn't at all sure he'd make the trade.

Except it didn't happen. Pat leaned over the guy, who didn't move, and then she turned and called back up to Grofield, "He's unconscious!"

"You're too damn lucky!" he yelled at her. "Go get Jack's gun. And for Christ's sake, stay out of my line of fire."

"Don't worry, don't worry."

At least she did that part right. She circled around to Jack's other side and took the gun from his uncomplaining hand. She already had the other one from the guy Grofield had shot.

Just as she was straightening up with Jack's gun the rain came, a sudden fusillade of rain, a drenching immediate downpour that hit the ground as though it had been dumped out of a bucket. Little gusts of rain puffed in Grofield's glassless window, polka-dotting the steps, and in the first violence of the rain he couldn't make out anything clearly out there. There was a movement out there, movement around Pat, but what was it?

He left the window and went bounding down the steps and out into the rain, in time to see Pat and Jack spinning around like a couple waltzing to frug music. Grofield dashed out into the rain, but when he got there Jack was lying on the ground again and Pat was standing there with two guns in her hands, like Annie Oakley.

"What happened?" He had to shout to be heard over the roar of the rain. They both looked like drowned cats.

"He tried to get the gun away from me," she shouted back. A car drove by, inched by, out on the road, the occupants not seeing a thing of what was happening in front of the tower.

"I know that," Grofield shouted back. "What did you do?"

"I hit him with it!"

Grofield went down on one knee. Jack had a gash on his forehead, but it was impossible to tell whether it was bleeding or not, with all the rainwater washing over his head.

"We've got to roll them over!" Grofield shouted. "So they don't drown!"

"What?"

"Roll him over!" Grofield bellowed and ran to do the same for the other one, rolling him face down and then taking a look for the wound.

It had been a pretty good shot, catching him in the fatty part of the leg, just above the left knee. It didn't look as though any bones were broken, but the slug was a large one, thrown by a gun with a lot of power behind it, and the skin was badly broken and bruised in an area around the wound the size of a pancake.

The rain was beginning to slacken. Grofield picked up the wounded man and lugged him over to the Pontiac. Pat was already there, with the door open, and Grofield eased the body onto the back seat. "Tie him tight," he said, and Pat nodded, and he went back for Jack.

Jack was on hands and knees, shaking his head. Grofield prodded him with the gun barrel, saying, "On your feet." The rain had eased enough now so he could be heard without shouting.

Jack was very slow in coming to full consciousness. Either that, or he wanted Grofield to think he was slow. Grofield stayed back, too far away to be jumped, and finally Jack got to his feet and stood swaying there. The rain was fading fast, down to a drizzle by now, with breeze-tossed misting.

"Over to the Pontiac," Grofield told him.

They used Jack's necktie to tie his hands behind his back. Pat had already trussed the man in the back seat, using his tie and belt and shoelaces. Grofield helped Jack into the passenger side of the front seat, then tied his ankles with his shoelaces and belt.

Jack said one thing: "I don't know what you're up to, pal, but I think you're crazy."

"So do I," Grofield told him.

The rain had stopped now. Grofield went around to the driver's side of the Pontiac, got in, and backed the car almost onto the road, then steered it over to the far corner of the parking area, where no other car was likely to park near it.

There was a box of tissues on the floor in back. Grofield grabbed a few tissues, wadded them in a ball, and said, "Open your mouth."

"Go to hell," Jack said.

Grofield hit him in the stomach, not very hard, and said, "You want to lie here in a lot of vomit?"

Jack opened his mouth.

Grofield stuffed the tissues in. Jack would be able to spit them out in time, but time was all Grofield was hoping for. He packed the unconscious man's mouth with tissues, too, then opened the driver's door, grabbed Jack by the collar, and as he backed out he pulled Jack down till he was lying across the seat.

Grofield went around to the other side, opened the door, and put Jack's feet up on the seat. Then he rolled up that window and closed and locked that door.

Back around on the driver's side, he reversed the automatic, took aim, and tapped Jack on the back of the head, pulling it a little because he didn't want to do any permanent damage. Jack made a noise, and when Grofield looked at his face he was still conscious, wincing from the pain. It hadn't been quite hard enough.

"Sorry," Grofield said, and tapped him again, doing it right this time. Then he rolled up the window on the driver's side, took the keys from the ignition, shut and locked the door.

Pat was already in the Mercedes when Grofield got back to it. He slid in behind the wheel, found the key in the ignition, and started the engine. "Set," he said.

"I didn't think it would work," she said. "I was terrified. I thought a million things would go wrong."

"Like you running out there when I told you not to."

"I'm sorry. When you shot him, I just thought oh, no, somebody's going to be killed."

"It could have been you and me."

"I know. I'll try to do better next time."

"That's good," Grofield said, and backed the Mercedes around in a tight turn. A car with two young couples in it pulled in on his right, stopped, and the couples got out and went into the tower. They looked with some curiosity at the Mercedes, but they paid no attention to the Pontiac at all.

"I'm freezing," she said.

"That's because you're wet."

"I know why I'm freezing," she said, hugging herself. "I'm still freezing whether I know why or not."

Grofield switched on the heater. "We should dry fast," he said.

"Everytime I go anywhere with you I get soaked," she said.

He laughed. "One way or the other." He steered the car down the road, back the way they'd come.

25

"Y o u don't think it was Roy, do you?"

Grofield looked at her. "I don't think what was Roy?"

"The killer."

Grofield made a disgusted face, saying, "Will you get off my back about that?"

"If you didn't want me to ask," she said, "you shouldn't have mentioned it. After all, what do you expect me to do?"

"All right," Grofield said. "I'll tell you. But I won't talk about it, I won't justify it, I won't say anything more about it at all. Is that fair?"

"Perfectly fair," she said. "Just tell me who."

He told her.

Pat said, "What? You're kidding!"

They had driven the Mercedes back down out of the mountains, the five miles back to route 3, where they'd turned left and gone about half a mile before Grofield found a broad dirt stretch to pull off the road into. It hadn't rained down here, of course, and the temperature was edging eighty-five, the sun climbing close to zenith, the air heavy with sunshine and heat. They'd gotten out of the car to walk around in the sun a little bit and dry their clothing, and they could practically see the steam rising from their clothes as they walked around.

Now, Pat said, "You are kidding, aren't you?"

"I knew it," Grofield said, and turned away and went back to the car. He pulled open the driver's door.

Pat hadn't moved. She said, "You mean you aren't kidding?"

"I told you," he said, "I wasn't going to justify, or explain, or prove it, or anything else. Get in the car."

"My underthings are still wet. Alan, are you *sure?*"

"You'd have to take your blouse and skirt off to get them dry," Grofield told her. "I've got the same problem." His socks had refused to dry, also, so he'd taken them off, and the un-accustomed feeling of sockless feet in his shoes—particularly in wet shoes—was irritating him, making him shorter of temper than he might have been otherwise.

"You really aren't going to talk about it, are you?" she said. "I think that's mean."

"Come on," Grofield said impatiently. "Get in the car. Let's get this damn thing over with."

She came sulkily around to her side of the car and got in. They shut their doors and Grofield started the engine. There wasn't quite as much traffic westbound, toward San Juan, but what there was took its time, and with the endless stream coming the other way it was impossible ever to pass anybody. Grofield got into line and drove along at the forty miles an hour that seemed to be standard here. He had about eight miles before the turn-off at Loiza.

They traveled about a mile in silence, and then Pat said, "I think you're wrong."

Grofield didn't say anything.

"Did you hear me? I say I think you're wrong."

"You're entitled to your opinion," he said, watching the road.

She glared at him. "You're infuriating," she said. "Do you know that? You're infuriating."

"You were better off before I told you," he said. "You should have let it alone, the way I wanted."

"You can at least *talk* about it."

"No. I have to think about what comes next here." He glanced at her, to let her know he was serious. "That's the important thing," he said. "What comes next. Not whodunit. I don't care whodunit. I care about being ready for what comes next, so I'll live through it."

She didn't say anything to that, not for another two miles, and when at last she did say something her manner was subdued: "I'm sorry," she said. "You're right."

He smiled at her and patted her knee. "Good girl," he said, mostly because he wanted her chipper, not gloomy, when they stormed the citadel. "After this is all over," he said, "you and I we'll go to bed with the head colds we're bound to have, and we'll talk about the killing of Belle Danamato for hours."

"The hell we will," she said.

26

"You all right back there?" Grofield said.

"Fine," she told him. "Ready to go."

They were on 185, about a mile from the turn-off to the house. Pat was in the back, down on the floor between the seats, holding one of the captured guns. Grofield had showed her how to work it, and she claimed she now understood. He had the automatic in his lap as he sat at the wheel, with the other captured pistol on the seat beside him.

It was just after noon. Tree branches roofed the road in shade, but it was still hot under here, hot and muggy. The mountains were ahead; pasture land was on both sides; there was a heavy midsummer stillness everywhere, as though all the world were indoors somewhere, taking a siesta, save only Grofield and Pat.

And Danamato, of course. And Danamato's soldiers, of course.

Grofield put the Mercedes in gear, and they slid forward. He was banking a lot on surprise, banking a lot on doing things they didn't expect him to do. They surely didn't expect him to come back to the house, not once he'd managed to get away from the damn place. And even more than that, they didn't expect to see him in their own black Mercedes. So if there was anybody on watch down by the turn-off and they saw the familiar black Mercedes coming in, they probably wouldn't look very hard at who was behind the wheel.

Maybe.

Grofield thought of it as a variant on the Trojan horse, and if it worked as well as the original he wouldn't mind a bit. If it didn't work, it was nice to know that this particular Trojan horse could travel at better than a hundred miles an hour.

The turn-off was ahead. "Here we go," Grofield called.

"Okay," she answered. There was hardly any tremor in her voice at all.

Grofield made the left. He remembered this from two days ago, when he'd come in here much more casually. The blacktop ended, the dirt road narrowed to one lane, it began to climb. The jungle growth got thicker, heavier, damper, even greener.

Four-tenths of a mile. Up ahead was the last turn, to the right, two thin tire tracks leading off into the jungle. And just beyond the turn, filling the road Grofield was on and facing this way, was the white Volvo.

Grofield dug his chin into his neck, sat way back in the seat, trying to create as much shadow for himself as he could. He couldn't clearly make out the faces of the two men in the Volvo, so why should they have any better luck seeing him?

One of them waved, just as he was making the turn. He waved back, the Mercedes slapped through the overhanging leaves, and the Volvo could no longer be seen. Nor could its occupants any longer see him.

"We just passed the Volvo," Grofield said. There was no tremor in his voice at all, not a trace.

"*What?*"

"It's all right," he said. "They waved, and I waved back. They can't see us any more."

"My God," she whispered, and Grofield wasn't entirely sure whether it was an exclamation or a prayer.

The road first dipped, and then very steeply climbed, just as he remembered it. He drove up slowly, the engine straining somewhat at the steepness and the low speed, and at his first glimpse of white he stopped and let the car roll back a little bit. Then he hit the brakes, pulled on the emergency, and shut off the ignition.

"We're here," he said.

She sat up onto the seat behind him, leaning forward with her forearms just behind his head. "I don't see the house."

"It's there," he said. "Just out of sight."

"Oh, I believe you. What now?"

"Now," he said, "I wish to Christ you knew how to drive."

"I'm sorry," she said. "I wish I did, too. I'm going to learn, you know, when we get back to the States."

Grofield didn't know whether the plural pronoun referred to himself or her brother, but he was willing to assume it was the brother she had in mind. "Unfortunately," he said, "there's no time to teach you now. So we'll have to do it a more complicated way."

"What do I do?"

"You get out of the car. You take that gun, and you go into the underbrush over there, far enough in so if anybody comes along they won't see you, but you'll be able to see them. All right?"

"Good," she said. "Is that all?"

"No. If you do see somebody, one of Danamato's people, you fire the gun."

"At them?" She sounded shocked.

"Anywhere you want," he told her. "It's mostly so I can hear it."

"Oh! A signal to you."

"Right. And after that you just try to keep away from them. They'll probably go in after you, but they'll know you're armed and they'll think you're me and they'll move very slow."

"And you'll come and rescue me."

The answer to that was very complicated, depending on where Grofield was at the time, but he didn't think it would be good for her morale to try to explain the complexities of it to her, so he said, "That's right. You just keep away from them till I get here."

"That's what I'll do," she said.

"Good."

He opened the door and got out, then helped her out after him. She put her arms around him and her face up to be kissed and he kissed her, but his mind was on other things.

She smiled up at him. She said, "Whatever happens now, Alan, I want you to know I thank you."

"For what?" He looked around. "For this? Coming back to get Roy?"

"No," she said, still smiling. "For telling me it was time to quit feeling sorry for myself. It was time, and I'm glad somebody told me about it."

"Oh. Happy to oblige."

"And I won't go back," she said. "To the way I was before, I mean. Roy is going to be very shocked, you know."

"I wouldn't be surprised."

"He would." She released him and stepped back, and her smile was now a little coquettish, a little teasing. "One more thing," she said.

He was checking the safety of the gun he'd taken from Jack, a Smith & Wesson Regulation Police .38 caliber revolver, and it was off. He tried to look attentive to her. "What's that?" he said.

"I've seen you wince," she said, "a couple of times, when you thought I was planning to hang around you after this is over. I just want you to know, you don't have to worry. I'm very fond of you, and I'm very grateful to you, but I just don't think you're husband material. Not for me, anyway. I'd get too nervous around you after a while."

He returned her smile. "I'm no place to live," he said, "but I'm a great place to visit."

"That's right."

"So I'll go get your brother now," he said. He pointed. "You get over in there."

"Yes, sir."

Grofield patted her cheek and turned away, and walked on

up the road toward the house, leaving the Mercedes behind him, facing uphill, blocking the road for any other vehicle that might want to come up here.

He hoped he could do this fast. In and out fast—that was the only way. They'd have the Volvo on their tails when they got out of here, of course, but the Mercedes should be able to take care of that.

And afterward? It was a big island. He could lie low for a while, or maybe take the boat over to the Virgin Islands, over to St. Thomas, and take a plane out of there somewhere else in the Caribbean, and thus eventually get back to the States again.

With no more side trips.

It was hard to believe how long he'd been away. He and a guy named Parker and a few other people had gone after that gambling casino on the island off Texas, the job had turned sour, he and Parker had traveled by boat from there to the Mexican coast, and from there on it had been nothing but one interruption after another. He hadn't planned on being out of the States at all, and here he was traveling all over Latin America.

Well, it would be over soon. One way or another, it would be over soon.

Up ahead was the house. Grofield moved to the edge of the cleared area, looked out there, saw no cars parked in front, no people moving around. He headed to the left, keeping in the shadow of the jungle growth, moving at a crouch, his feet distracting him without socks in his shoes.

It was stupid to be distracted by sockless feet at a time like this. He forced his mind to concern itself with what was important.

The left rear corner of the house seemed the nearest to the uncleared jungle. Grofield traveled around the perimeter until he was as close as he could get to that part of the house, then poised, looked at all the windows he could see without spying any faces looking out, and dashed for the corner of the house, running doubled, weaving, head low, silent and fast.

He reached the house, edged along it to a window, peered

in. A sitting room, of which the house was full, this one currently empty. Farther along, French doors led into that room. Grofield tried one, it was unlocked, he slipped quickly into the house.

So far so good.

Now all that was left to do was find Roy Chelm, take care of his guards if he was guarded, break open his door if it was locked, untie him if he was tied up, in any case find him and get him moving, get him out of the house without anyone seeing them leave, get him across the clearing and around the perimeter and into the Mercedes, get Pat into the Mercedes, back the Mercedes down to where the Volvo is waiting and where the Mercedes could be quickly turned around and gotten the hell out of there.

Simple.

If Roy Chelm was still alive.

He'd thought about that from time to time, without mentioning it to Pat. He hadn't mentioned it to her because in the first place she wouldn't believe him; she'd merely think he was trying to wangle a way out of this mess for himself, and also because in the second place he thought it unlikely. Danamato was surely very mad at Roy Chelm, for a number of reasons, and it wasn't at all unlikely that Danamato had slugged Chelm once or twice on his return to this house, but Danamato had no real reason to kill Chelm. Not unless he failed to get his hands on Grofield again, of course, in which instance he might kill Chelm just out of frustration.

But that point wouldn't have arrived yet, or shouldn't have arrived yet. Chelm should still be alive, and somewhere in these hundreds of rooms. Now all Grofield had to do was find him.

Silently he crossed the room, hesitated with his hand on the doorknob, finally pulled it open, and found himself looking into the surprised eyes of Onum Marba.

27

"N o t a sound," Grofield whispered. He showed Marba one of his guns, the 9mm automatic. The revolver was tucked away in his hip pocket.

"Of course not," Marba whispered back. After that one second of surprise, Marba had turned poker-faced again, his expression blank, his eyes bland, his arms quietly at his sides. He was dressed in his native robes, as he had been the first time Grofield had seen him.

Grofield took a step backward. "Come on in," he whispered, motioning to Marba with his free hand.

Marba stepped forward across the threshold.

"Shut the door," Grofield whispered.

"Certainly," Marba whispered. Not turning, he reached out his left hand and shut the door. Then he stood there, apparently totally at ease, and waited for whatever Grofield would tell him to do next.

Grofield no longer whispered, but he did speak quietly, saying, "You have nothing to fear from me as long as I have nothing to fear from you."

"That's reasonable," Marba said. "I will make no attempt to sound the alarm, I promise you."

"Good. Take a seat."

"Thank you."

While Marba settled himself in a chair of maroon mohair, adjusting his robes around his knees, Grofield backed away to the French doors and looked through the glass at the lawn and the jungle and the driveway. No one in sight.

Marba said, "You seem constantly amazing, Mr. Grofield. I never expected you here again of your own free will."

"Not exactly my free will," Grofield said. "How many are in the house?"

"How many gunmen, you mean?"

"How many anybody."

"Of guests," Marba said, "three. The Milfords and myself. I suppose Mr. Danamato must be counted host. Of his associates, four, including poor Harry, who is bedridden upstairs. You seem to have done something terrible to his nose."

"I'm sorry about that."

The hint of a smile flickered in Marba's vicinity. "I had thought you would be. Finally, of prisoners, one. Roy Chelm. In your old accommodations."

"Upstairs?"

Marba shook his head. "Downstairs."

"Guarded?"

"I believe not. When I last saw Mr. Danamato's assistants, they were playing cards in the east dining room."

"All three?"

"Four. Mr. Danamato was with them."

Grofield glanced out the window. Still no one out there. Still no sound of a shot.

Would he hear it if it came while he was down in the basement?

He turned back to Marba. "What about the two natives?" he said. "The one with the shotgun and the one with the dog."

"Gone. All the servants are gone." Marba perhaps thought of

smiling again. "Mrs. Milford has been kind enough to prepare our meals since they left."

"Danamato sent them away?"

"Not directly."

Grofield shook his head. "What does that mean?"

Now Marba did smile, briefly but clearly. "I'm sorry," he said. "Speaking obliquely becomes a habit, hard to break. The servants seemed frightened of Mr. Danamato and his friends. Perhaps just frightened of the situation here. In any event, they ran away."

"Where are the Milfords?"

"I'm not sure. Somewhere about the house. Probably not together."

"Why not?"

Marba shrugged slightly, so slightly as to barely disturb his robes. "They seem to have been avoiding one another lately," he said. "I have no idea why."

There were no more questions to ask, and time was short. Grofield said, "The problem is, what do I do now with you?"

"Me? You could leave me here, right where I am."

Grofield considered him. "I'd rather be sure you were safe."

"Trussed up in a closet somewhere?" Marba's impassive face managed to convey humorous self-pity. "I would prefer not, if we could avoid it. Can you take my word for it that my word can be taken?"

"That's the problem, isn't it?"

"I guarantee not to inform on you," Marba said. "You can trust me, though I have no idea how to convince you of that."

Grofield looked out the window, looked back at Marba. The major reason to take a chance on Marba was the need for speed. "I trust you," Grofield said. "I think you're a man of honor."

Marba laughed, an amazing performance, his poker face breaking open entirely into something sweet and kind. "Even if I weren't," he said, "I would have to be one now. Mr. Grofield, I acknowledge the presence of another politician." He bowed his head, still smiling.

"Thank you," Grofield said.

"I wish you luck. And it would please me if we were to meet again."

Grofield returned his smile this time. "Me too," he said, and meant it. He glanced one last time out the window, then headed for the door. "See you later."

"Under happier circumstances. Goodbye, Mr. Grofield."

Grofield put his hand on the knob "Goodbye, Mr. Marba."

The corridor was clear. Grofield went out, shut the door behind him, and flitted along the corridor on the balls of his feet, pausing at every open doorway, hurrying as fast as silence would permit.

He met no one until just before he reached the closed door to the basement stairs. He was three or four steps from there when he saw the doorknob turn, saw the door start to open.

There was an open door on his left, leading to a small light room dominated by a sewing machine and a dressmaker's form. Grofield ducked in there, pressed himself against the wall beside the doorway, and listened.

He heard Eva Milford's voice: " . . . eat any better than that. I think it's criminal to keep that boy down there. Criminal. What has he done?"

A male voice grunted, without words.

"I'm going to speak to Mr. Danamato again." The voice was trailing away down the hall, and Grofield, peeking out, saw Eva Milford carrying a tray, with Danamato's man Frank walking along beside her.

The two made the turn and were gone.

Grofield came out of the sewing room, paused, listened, heard nothing, and moved quickly to the basement door. It was shut again. He opened it, found the light switch inside, clicked on the light, and stepped in, shutting the door again behind him.

It was too bad about the door. He'd have preferred to leave it part way open, in case there was a shot to be heard. But it was kept normally closed, and anyone passing would notice if it were not. Notice and possibly investigate.

It was bad enough he had to leave the light on.

He hurried down the stairs into the damp coolness of the

basement. Rough gray walls formed a large open square room, from which low-ceilinged corridors led away to left and right. Grofield turned left, toward the room Harry had put him in after Belle Danamato's murder. There was another light switch on the wall, and when he clicked it the corridor formed itself in yellow light from three bare bulbs of low wattage spaced along the ceiling.

There were a number of shut doors along the corridor on both sides, with Grofield's old cell being the third on the left. Like the others, this door was thick and heavy and massive, built of old dark wood. Unlike the others, this one was locked.

Three times locked. There were two bolts, one near the top of the door and one near the bottom, and both were slid into place. By the handle there was a hasp and padlock.

They must have had a higher opinion of Roy Chelm than Grofield.

Grofield slid back the two bolts, but the padlock was going to be another problem. The key wasn't around, of course, and a tentative rattling of the lock showed it was indeed shut.

Tools. Grofield looked around, then started searching the other rooms down here. He needed tools, some kind of tools.

The third room he tried was pay dirt. It was a hobbyist's dream room, a small square full of every tool a do-it-yourselfer has ever dreamed of. Power tools were lined up on shelves to the left. A workbench with drawers stood on the right. And on a pegboard straight ahead hung every imaginable kind of saw, wrench, pliers, screwdriver and hammer.

Grofield went over, smiling, selected himself a heavy screwdriver, turned out the light, shut the door from the outside, and went back to Roy Chelm's prison. He was very nearly whistling.

But it wasn't going to be that easy. He'd chosen the longest and heaviest screwdriver in the collection because he intended to use it as a crowbar, prying the hasp loose from either the door or the doorframe, but the damn thing just didn't want to pry. He braced elbows and knees against the door, tucked the screwdriver in behind the flat of the hasp and pulled, and nothing happened.

The problem was, he couldn't get at the screws. The flat of the hasp covered them all. He tugged and yanked, but it wasn't budging at all.

Hell.

He'd wanted to do it the quiet way, but apparently it wasn't to be. He finally gave up when his hands got slippery enough to begin sliding on the handle of the screwdriver. He went back to the workroom, turned on the light, returned the screwdriver to its place on the pegboard, and selected a heavy hammer in its stead, a twenty-ouncer ball peen.

In a workbench drawer he found some old rags and brought one of them along, too. Back he went to the padlocked door. He slipped the rag through the padlock, to muffle the sound somewhat, took aim, and slammed downward at the edge of the padlock with the peen side of the hammer.

The *kang!* seemed to fill the cellar. Had it been heard upstairs? For all he knew, he was standing directly underneath where Danamato and his boys were playing cards.

And the lock hadn't broken.

Impatient, enraged, beginning to get frightened, he grimaced like Kirk Douglas and hit it again, and this time the lock popped open like a dead pretzel.

About time. He put the hammer on the floor, slipped the padlock out of the ring, slid the hasp free, turned the knob, and opened the door.

Roy Chelm looked at him with blank astonishment. "What in the name of God are you doing here?"

"Your sister sent me to get you. Come on."

Chelm didn't move. "My sister?"

"She's waiting for us outside. Come on."

Chelm's astonishment was turning to fear now, and he looked behind Grofield as though expecting to see Danamato and a cast of thousands back there. "Are you crazy?" he said, his voice hushed. "We'll never get out of here!"

"Sure we will." Grofield's guns were both in his hip pockets, and he now took them both out, the 9mm automatic in his right hand, the .38 revolver in his left. "Your sister's in the car," he said. "We don't have any time to waste. If somebody starts to chase us, just shoot this thing. Not at them, just shoot, just so they hear the noise." He handed the .38 to Chelm.

Chelm took the gun in a dazed sort of way, looked at it, then used it to hit Grofield on the right wrist, knocking the automatic out of his hand.

"Ow!"

Chelm stepped quickly back a pace, the revolver pointed at Grofield. "Hands up," he said.

28

GROFIELD held his wrist with his other hand. He was disgusted. He said, "You're nuts, Chelm. This is pointless."

"Is it?"

"I could get you out of here."

"This way is surer," Chelm said, smiling briskly. "And safer. For Patricia *and* me."

"Pat won't thank you for this," Grofield warned him.

Chelm's smile turned superior. "You really think so? You really think Patricia would take any interest in a roustabout like you?"

"Yes."

"I imagine she did have to treat you more civilly than she would have liked," Chelm said cozily, "in order to get you to come in here after me, but I hate to disillusion you. Her attitude toward you is not one iota different from mine."

"You're such a clown," Grofield said. He shook his head. "You're such an out-and-out clown."

"We'll see about that. Back up a pace. Two paces."

Grofield moved back two paces. It put him not quite close enough to the door.

Would Chelm shoot? Yes, Grofield thought gloomily, the moron probably would shoot. And with beginner's luck, he'd get Grofield in the middle of the head.

Chelm came forward, squatted carefully, keeping his eyes and gun pointed at Grofield, and picked up the automatic with his other hand. He straightened again and now he had two guns. Standing there, pointing them at Grofield, he looked like a sloppy parody of Billy the Kid.

"What now?" Grofield asked him.

"Now," Chelm said, "we go upstairs, where I turn you over to your friend Danamato."

Grofield sighed. "That's what I thought."

Chelm smiled a smile that demanded to be wiped off. "You really are a help," he said. "I give you to Danamato, who is then grateful to me and has no longer any reason to hold me prisoner. He releases me, and Patricia and I return to the States."

"With my blood on your hands," Grofield told him, knowing it wouldn't make any difference.

It didn't. "On Danamato's hands," Chelm said blithely. "Besides, you already have his wife's blood on yours."

"You know I don't."

"Do I? Turn around, Grofield."

Grofield turned around. He hunched his shoulders automatically, expecting a gun butt on his skull, but that wasn't the way Chelm was going to play it, either because he didn't want to handle it the safe way or because it didn't occur to him. Probably it didn't occur to him.

"Walk," said Chelm.

Grofield walked. His hands were up, Chelm stayed far enough behind him, there was nothing to do.

They got to the foot of the stairs. If there was going to be a chance, it was here. Either Chelm would get too close to him on the stairs and give Grofield a shot at knocking him down, or he'd stay too far away and give Grofield a shot at getting out the door and away.

But no. Not that either. Behind him, Chelm said, "That's far enough. Don't go up the stairs. And don't turn around!"

Grofield had been about to. He stopped the movement and stayed where he was. What now?

"Turn left," Chelm said.

That was away from the stairs. Grofield turned, his back to the stairs now.

"Take three paces," Chelm told him.

Grofield took three paces. That put him in the middle of the square room, too far away from everything.

"Good," Chelm said, and raised his voice to shout, "Help!"

Grofield looked over his shoulder at him. "You're a goddam fool, Chelm," he said.

"We'll see. Help! Danamato! Down in the cellar!"

Feet could be heard running upstairs, thudding along above their heads.

Grofield said, "Your sister will curse the day you were born. She'll never forgive you the rest of your life."

"Oh, don't be silly, you ragamuffin. Danamato! Down here!"

The door burst open at the head of the stairs. Frank and the bearded man jumped into view, stared down at the two of them, and Frank said, "Well, for Christ's sake!"

They came rushing down the stairs. Grofield turned around now, but kept his hands up, and watched them come. It was all over.

Frank was just astounded, but the bearded man thought it was too funny to be believed. "Well, you little love!" he said to Grofield, laughing in his face. "You've come home!"

Chelm handed the guns over to Frank, saying, "These are his guns. I don't believe he has any more."

Snickering, the bearded man said to Grofield, "Did little Roy take your guns away all by himself? Both of them?"

"I thought he was on my side," Grofield said.

"Oh, that's sad," the bearded man said, and roared with laughter.

They marched him upstairs, Frank going first, Grofield second, the bearded man chuckling along third, and Roy Chelm happily coming last.

In the upstairs hall Frank and the bearded man took Grofield's arms and walked him down the hall. They passed Marba in one doorway, who gave Grofield a slight sympathetic nod on the way by.

They turned to the left, down another hall, and into a room where cards were on the table.

Danamato got to his feet. "It is you, you bastard," he said, and hit Grofield flush in the mouth with all his strength.

29

GROFIELD felt a hand very gentle on his forehead. He opened his eyes and saw Pat Chelm smiling very sadly at him. Beyond her was a ceiling.

He moved his head, which was lying on something soft. "What . . . "

"Easy," she said, and touched her hands to his face again, and he realized he was lying on the floor with his head in her lap.

He lifted his head slightly and saw he was still in the room where the boys had been playing cards. Far away near the windows, Danamato was talking to the three boys. A little nearer, looking bewildered, Roy Chelm was leaning against the wall and holding a bloodied handkerchief to his face. He met Grofield's eyes and quickly looked away again.

Grofield let his head lie back on Pat's lap. "What happened to your brother?

"I hit him," she said, her tone stern.

"With what, for God's sake?"

"With the gun you gave me. You wouldn't believe how pompous he came out to get me. He'd solved everything, he'd worked everything out, he'd turned you over to Danamato and now we were safe."

"I know," Grofield said. "From his point of view, I suppose it made sense."

"Why not?" she said, voice low but angry. "All sorts of things can make sense to a moron."

Grofield grinned despite himself. "I tried to tell him you wouldn't be pleased," he said.

"He knows it now, the stupid creep." She suddenly bent low over him, her near breast grazing his chin. "Oh, Alan, I am sorry! If I'd known just how big a fool Roy was, I would never have gotten you into this. I'd have left him here to rot."

"Me too," Grofield said. "Where's that gun of yours now?"

"They took it away from me."

"Too bad."

Danamato, from across the room, suddenly called, "Is the bastard awake?"

"No," she said, too fast and too loud. "He's still unconscious."

"The hell he is." Danamato came stomping over and glared down at Grofield. "He's awake, all right."

Grofield made as though he were just coming to consciousness: "Where . . . where am I?"

"You know where you are, you bastard. And I know where you're going."

"But the devil knows who I'll marry," Grofield murmured.

"What?"

"He can't get up yet," Pat said. Her arms went around his head. "He's still too dizzy."

"You're the dizzy one," Danamato told her. "On your feet, Grofield, you can walk. You won't be goin' far, anyway."

She kept her arms around his head. "Tell him, Alan," she said urgently. "Tell him the truth."

"What difference would it make?" Grofield said. "Let me up, Pat."

She wouldn't, not yet. "It's your only chance," she insisted. "You've got to *try*, you've got to at least *try*."

"What's all this crap?" Danamato wanted to know.

She looked up at him. "Alan knows who really did kill your wife."

Danamato grinned. "Sure. Him."

"No!"

Grofield told her wearily, "Forget it, Pat, he won't listen."

"To a lot of crap?" Danamato demanded. "This guy gave it away on himself when he ran away from here. If he was innocent he'd 've stuck around."

"To be killed?" Pat glared up at Danamato. "You already had your mind set against him. You were giving it a little time because he'd managed to make you do *some* thinking, but in the end you were going to take the easy way out and you know it. Alan ran away because you were going to kill him, not because he was guilty."

Danamato shook his head. "Forget it, little girl," he said. "It's nice to know you two had fun together on your vacation, but it's all over. Get on your feet, Grofield."

Grofield disengaged Pat's arms and sat up. "Coming, Mother," he said.

Pat said, "*Please*, Alan! *Tell* him!"

"He won't believe me," Grofield told her, beginning to lose patience. "I can't prove it, and he won't believe it. He wouldn't believe it if the killer walked in here and admitted it. He's got me, and I'm all he wants."

"You're all I need," Danamato said. "Up, Grofield."

Grofield used a handy chair to help him get to his feet. He looked at Pat, and he thought about what he'd just said, and he said, "Maybe." He sat down in the chair.

"What now?" Danamato shouted.

"Bring them in here," Grofield told him. "If the real killer speaks up, you'll let me go. If nobody speaks up, that's tough on me."

"More games? Why should I play more games with you, Grofield?"

"Because you want to be sure," Pat told him quickly. She was standing beside Grofield, her hand on his shoulder. "I know he's innocent, and he knows he's innocent, and you half suspect he's innocent."

"The hell!"

"He wants one chance," Pat said. "What can it cost you to give him one chance?"

Danamato gnawed his cheeks. He brooded over Grofield, studying him sitting in the chair, and finally said, "Two minutes. You get two minutes." Then he turned to his soldiers and called, "Bring everybody in here!" Looking back at Grofield, he said, "You want Harry?"

"No. Harry didn't do it."

"That's a change for you, Grofield. The last time you were pushing Harry down my throat."

"I didn't know who really was guilty then."

"But you do now," Danamato said with heavy sarcasm.

"Yes."

Marba came in, looked at Grofield, looked at Chelm, and said mildly, "This house seems bad for noses. I hope mine isn't next."

Nobody answered him.

The Milfords came in together, both wary looking, followed by Danamato's men.

Danamato said to Grofield, "Your two minutes just started."

Grofield carefully looked at no one. His eyes looking at a point on the rug, he said, "What Mr. Danamato means, in two minutes I'm going to be taken out of here, walked off into the jungle, and shot. That's going to happen because he thinks I killed his wife. I know who did kill his wife—"

Someone made a small noise.

"—but I can't prove it, and he won't believe me without proof. But he'd believe a confession from the real killer. That's the only thing that will keep me from being taken out and shot, if the real killer speaks up and tells the truth."

He stopped then and waited, and nobody said anything. He sighed and said, "How much time have I got, Danamato?"

"One minute five seconds."

Still looking at the rug, Grofield said, "Look at it this way. Danamato will kill me for killing his wife, but he won't do anything to you. Don't you realize that? He won't touch you. Maybe the law will, maybe you'll go to jail, but Danamato won't touch you. And you won't have a second killing on your conscience."

He waited again, and again there was silence. He went on: "I know you don't want me to be shot for your crime. That's why you helped me once. But I need more help than that. I need you to speak up."

Nothing. No one.

Grofield shook his head. "How much time, Danamato?"

"Twenty seconds."

"Not much time."

"You bought yourself two extra minutes of life, Grofield," Danamato said, "but they're just about run out."

Grofield looked up. "Mrs. Milford," he said, "aren't you going to speak up?"

Mrs. Milford looked at him, impassive, silent.

Her husband said, "What? Are you out of your mind, Grofield?"

Danamato shouted, "God damn it, all you want to do is die a smart-ass! Get on your feet, Grofield!"

Grofield stayed where he was. He said to Danamato, "Let me tell you about it." And then hurried on, before Danamato could say yes or no. "We were right about me being hired for more than just public bodyguard. Belle had been doing the celibacy bit for Roy's sake for a month, and she was sick of it. She was beginning to realize there was nothing in it for her and Roy, this escapade was running its course. She'd already told Milford she wasn't going to be investing after all."

"She told me," Milford corrected him, "that she wouldn't be investing in Marba's casino."

"She wasn't ready to go back to you yet," Grofield went on, ignoring the interruption, "but she was ready to kick celibacy. Chelm had her going for a month, which was probably a long time for her—"

Danamato made a small grunt of laughter.

"—but Chelm is good at that kind of supermoral influence. Ask his sister."

"That's true!" Pat cried. "I was miserable trying to be what Roy wanted me to be, and I never knew why!"

"Pat!" Chelm cried, his voice muffled by the handkerchief he still held to his face.

Mrs. Milford continued to watch Grofield and say nothing.

Grofield told Danamato, "She wanted a man. Nobody around seemed to her to fill the bill, with the possible exception of George Milford, but he'd already told her he was being on his best behavior with his wife around, and it would have been too complex an affair to get involved in with her here anyway."

Milford said, "Be careful how you speak of the dead, Grofield. Have a little respect."

Danamato said, "Let him go. I like the way he makes this stuff up as he goes along. He was doing the same jazz the other day, one of you people after the other."

"But this is the real one," Grofield said. "Because when I got here and I didn't work out, in fact your wife and I didn't get along at all, she was very disappointed. And she went after Milford that night."

"The man's out of his mind!" Milford shouted.

Grofield looked at him. "You've known it was your wife did it all along. Every step of the way, you knew it was her."

"I can understand your desperation," Milford told him, "but I would have thought even a man like you would draw the line somewhere."

"Nowhere," Grofield told him. He said to Danamato, "Milford didn't fool his wife. She'd been expecting it, I suppose. So when her husband got back to his own bed he was probably there, to give him the word. He told her he'd been seduced or something, he couldn't help it, it was that old weakness of his again, Belle Danamato brought out the worst in him, some kind of crap like that, and off she went to see Belle and tell her to lay off her husband."

"I don't want to hear any more of this," Milford said, "and neither does my wife." He took Eva Milford's arm, as though to leave the room.

"Wait around," Danamato told him. "Go on, Grofield. I like the way you talk, you're a lot of fun."

Grofield told him, "Your wife could be an arrogant bitch sometimes, Danamato. She got me riled from a standing start. Mrs. Milford went in there already riled. It didn't take long to get up to murder." He turned to Eva Milford. "Did it, Mrs. Milford?"

Her face continued expressionless; she continued to have nothing to say.

"Actually," Grofield said, directly to her now, "it wasn't Belle you wanted to kill. It was your husband, or maybe that high-school girl back home. But Belle was the one who got all the frustration, first with an ashtray or something on the head and then with the wire wrapped around the neck. But you didn't want me to pay for something you did, so you talked the Chelms into running away and taking me with them. But I'm back now, and I am going to pay for your crime unless you speak up."

Milford had his arm around his wife's shoulders. "My wife has nothing to say," he said loudly.

"Danamato wouldn't lay a hand on you," Grofield told Eva Milford. "You know that, don't you? The worst he'd do is turn you over to the police."

There was silence. Grofield kept looking at Eva Milford. She returned his gaze expressionlessly. Everyone waited.

When Danamato broke the silence at last, he seemed almost disappointed. "Well, Grofield," he said, "it was a nice try. Keep everybody confused, maybe it'll work out to your advantage somewhere along the line. But not this time. Help Mr. Grofield to his feet, boys."

Pat lunged at Danamato and had to be held back. Marba seemed on the verge of saying something, but didn't.

Grofield got up. The bearded man opened a French door and beckoned. "Come along, honey," he said. "Let's us guys go for a walk in the woods."

Grofield walked over there. Maybe somewhere between here and the end of the line there'd be a chance, a moment, a possibility. It was unlikely, but it was all he had left.

"That's nice, love," said the bearded man. A revolver was in his hand, and his smile seemed made of stone.

Grofield reached the French doors, and Eva Milford said, "He told the truth."

Grofield leaned his shoulder against the doorjamb and shook his head. "It's about time," he told the bearded man.

30

"I think I'm done on that side," Pat said, and rolled over on the blanket to offer her front to the sun.

Beside her, Grofield stretched, realized he'd been dozing off, and sat up. "I'm going to take another dip," he said. "Want to come along?"

"No, thanks. I'm too lazy. I'll just lie here and broil."

"Right."

They were at Luquillo Beach, a long, flat, curving beach about thirty miles east of San Juan. Flat parkland dotted with tall palms stretched inland from the beach, sectioned with parking lots. There were probably lots of people out here today, but the beach was so long that there was no feeling of being in a crowd.

Grofield walked down to the water. A point of land way to the right protected this broad and shallow cove from the ocean waves, so that the water merely rippled beneath the sun. Back at San Juan, the ocean pounded a little too dangerously at the hotel beaches, but here the water was tame and mild.

And refreshing. Grofield dove in, and though the salt water stung his cut nose, it wasn't bad, not so bad as it had been two days ago, shortly after Danamato had hit him.

He swam out and back, out and back. He floated for a while, swam a while longer, then left the water and strolled lazily back to the blanket, where Pat was lying now face down again. Her tan was coming along very well. Better than Grofield's since she worked at it more consistently, while he spent a lot of his time in the water.

He lay down beside her, rolling on the blanket to semi-dry himself. He finished on his stomach and elbows and looked at his watch, lying on the corner of the blanket. "Three o'clock," he said.

She stirred. "Mm?"

"Three o'clock."

"Oh." She came up on her elbows, too, blinking and yawning. "I was just about asleep. Time for us to go?"

"Soon. My plane's at six."

She leaned over and kissed his shoulder, then smiled at him. "Who am I going to get to drive me out to this lovely lovely place after you leave?"

"You'll find someone," he said.

Her smile turned wicked. "You just bet I will," she said. "If only Roy could see you now."

"Roy!" His name could still get her angry. "If he ever comes back down here," she said, "I'll *kick* him to the States!"

"You aren't staying forever, are you?"

She shrugged. "Until I feel like going somewhere else," she said. "Roy will send me money. He feels he owes me."

"He owes *me*, the little twit," Grofield said.

She laughed. "I'll collect it for you."

"You do that." He looked at the watch again. "We ought to get going."

"We're only an hour from the hotel," she said.

"I know."

She looked at him. "Oh," she said. "You mean you want to say goodbye to me."

"That's right," he said.

"At the hotel."

"That's right," he said.

"Fondly. And for a long long time."

"That's right," he said.

"Like for two hours."

"At least," he said.

"Then we ought to get going," she said.